TUOYAWON

R. Murrey Haist

ISBN 978-1-64140-632-1 (paperback)
ISBN 978-1-64140-633-8 (digital)

Christian Faith Publishing, Inc.
832 Park Avenue
Meadville, PA 16335
www.christianfaithpublishing.com

Printed in the United States of America

CHAPTER

The moon shone bright against the somber, starless sky. Its light pierced through the trees that lined the lonely road. It was early spring, and the leaves had not yet come to the trees. The shadows cast were eerie and unsettling as they rushed toward her, resembling long knurled witch's fingers grasping and clutching at Chrissy's car.

The swamp residents had awakened, and their chirps and croaks echoed through the warm spring night. The sweet smell of new growth and marsh flowers wafted in the air. The scent of early spring and nature's rhapsody were all stimuli that would normally invigorate her. But Chrissy's life had abruptly taken a terrifying turn! She now barely noticed them as she stared unfocused on the road ahead, only paying close attention to her speed. Even though there was no one in sight, she did not want to draw attention to herself. All the time she was wondering, how it all came to this.

With her mind wondering over her former life—the life she led before today—she remembered her times at the family's lake retreat.

Her parents bought the cottage when she was just three years old. She remembered all the kids there, those lifelong friends that she grew up with. Sure, there were friends from school in town, and although they were close, it did not seem that they were as close as those at the lake.

Tommy was the same age as Chrissy. He was the adopted son of a couple two cottages away. Of all her friends, Tommy was the one she was always the closest to. Tommy was the one whom she shared her secrets with. He was the one she shared her first kiss with.

A reluctant smile came to her as she recalled the times when, each summer, the cottagers would get together and put on a bike derby. All the kids would decorate their bicycles and tricycles and dress themselves in funny costumes. They would then parade up and down the roads while the cottagers sat at the road's edge judging. The best dressed would win prize bags full of bike trinkets (like streamers, bells, and horns) and candies—lots of candies. It seemed that everyone won a prize bag!

She remembered the times goofing around with the group. Each would try to outdo the other by showing off how they could ride their bikes with great skill. She recalled how her hands-free stunt ended with her taking a header onto the gravel road. Although there were a lot of scrapes and scratches, there was never any real damage, just bruised pride.

Chrissy allowed a light inner snicker, thinking of her thirteenth birthday. What a big event that was! Her mom and dad had put together a weekend camp out party. They invited all her friends from the lake and her friends from town. The small cottage lot was a sea of tents.

She recalled how, when they saw Tommy coming with a pie plate with whipped cream, they all knew the intent was to bathe her face, and how they chased her for two blocks before they caught her.

All the fun, all the good times—where did they go? They seemed so long ago.

And then there was Ryan, and a whole new chapter opened in her life.

Chrissy quickly crashed back to the present with the sudden appearance of a coyote dashing across the road. She swerved to the right to miss it, only to find herself skidding around in the muddy shoulder. No matter how hard she tried to get her car back onto the road, the mire sucked her closer to the tree line.

After what seemed like twenty minutes of an off-road race in a shopping cart (the reality was probably just a few seconds), her car finally came to a stop—and, fortunately, just before an unpleasant meeting with a large oak tree. Had it been just a week later, the spring thaw may have been further along and given her firmer ground to maneuver.

Chrissy was stuck, alone, and with no idea where she was. And with her daydreams, she could not even remember if she had seen another car, or even a road sign, for the last hour.

Considering her options, she scanned the desolate road in both directions, determining it would be safer to stay with the car than walk a road that leads to who knows where at night with who knows what creatures might be out there.

As she became resigned to the fact of sleeping in her car until daylight, her mind wandered back to the first time she met Ryan.

She and her family had just returned from three weeks away at their cottage. They were unpacking the car when she first noticed him. She wondered why this cute guy was sitting on Mr. and Mrs. Norman's porch next door. Mrs. Norman had been ill for quite a long time, so she deduced he might be someone to help Mr. Norman with the yard work.

The Normans moved into the newly opened subdivision with their children about the same time as Chrissy's mom and dad. Their two children were their twelve-year-old son Howard and ten-year-old daughter Vivian. Mrs. Norman, Marian, was an avid gardener. As Chrissy's mother had grown up in the garden center atmosphere, they shared the same passion. Her mom and Mrs. Norman would spend the weekends working on landscape designs and coordinating plant products for their new barren lots. The homes of the Normans and Chrissy's parents soon became the talk of the small subdivision for their beautiful floral and shrub display and arrangements.

Three years after moving into this new home, Chrissy was born. In her very young years, Chrissy was babysat by the Normans' daughter, Vivian. She clearly recalled how she would stare admiringly at her babysitter and listened as she practiced her singing. A lot of the wonderful songs she sang, she had also written. To this day Chrissy could still, in her mind, hear that voice that was so sweet and smooth. Vivian's goal in life was to sing professionally, whether as a solo artist or as a lead in a group.

There were times when Chrissy would try to sing along. It was like an angel accompanied by a duck suffering with a bruised foot. No matter how off tune or out of sync Chrissy was, Vivian would always give a hug and say, "What a wonderful job."

Her brother Howard spent most of his time reading, and whenever Chrissy, as a young child, would visit the Normans next door, Howard would pull out a book and read to her.

Mrs. Norman loved to bake. No matter what the occasion at their home, whether it be a recital by Vivian or a reading by Howard, she would always serve up some of the most delicious treats.

This may have been where Chrissy first established her sweet tooth.

Mr. Norman was the principal at the local school but had retired when Chrissy was about four years old. He was a very kind, warmhearted man who could always be found with a smile and a kind gesture. He would spend most of his time in his garage building model airplanes. There were shelves filled with models of every size and shape as well as several hanging by string from the garage ceiling. Chrissy's brother Brad could often be found with Mr. Norman. All that time spent with Mr. Norman watching as he constructed the airplanes was probably the inspiration for Brad to want to become a pilot or join the Air Force.

When she was around eleven years old, Chrissy recalled, she was listening to the radio when she heard a familiar voice. That voice was the soloist who had entertained her as a younger child. Vivian had success with one of her songs, and although not world-renowned, over the years she had gained a very large local fan club.

Howard went on to teachers' college, became a teacher at an elementary school, and was married and with two children of his own.

Mrs. Norman fell ill with what they thought was just the flu, but she continued to become weaker and had remained in that condition for the past six years.

The car was almost unpacked from the three weeks away when Chrissy's dad called her and her brother together. He then announced, "Breaking but sad news—the Norman's house that had been for sale . . . Well, it sold just before we left for the lake. They have now retired to their cottage. The new people are already moved in. The good news is, we have new neighbors to welcome to our area."

Although curious, Chrissy, being a shy girl, did not want to appear too eager to meet this new neighbor. So as she made her last trips back and forth from the car to the house, striking all her best poses and being as noisy as she could, she grabbed quick glances of him. He did not even look up as he sat staring at something he was flipping around in his fingers.

After unloading the car, Chrissy's mother asked her and her younger brother to get cleaned up for supper, advising that she had invited the new neighbors over. This was to welcome them, have a barbecue, and get to know them.

Two hours later, the new neighbors arrived at the door and were introduced to Chrissy and her younger brother Brad.

Presenting a bottle of wine to her mom and dad, they identified Ryan as their fifteen-year-old son.

Chrissy, now thirteen and three-quarters, spent the whole afternoon shyly sneaking glimpses of this cute, new neighbor as he showed her eleven-year-old brother magic tricks with a coin he flipped between his fingers.

The afternoon went on, and at the end of the day, Chrissy's impression of Ryan was that although he was cute, he seemed very full of himself—in a quiet way.

Drifting back to the present, Chrissy rolled the windows all the way up. Double-checking the door locks, she reclined the car seat as she prepared to get some sleep.

A sudden banging and shouting shook Chrissy from her sleep!

"Are you okay?" came the shouts from outside the car window. "Can you hear me? Do I need to call for an ambulance?"

Startled and disoriented, she rubbed her eyes as she strained to focus out the window. In the shadow of the moonlight, she could make out the form of a man and behind him a car idling on the road.

Nervously, she cracked the window down just an inch, and a voice called out. "I am Reverend Sounders. Can I help you? Do you need an ambulance? Are you okay?"

Chrissy stammered a "Yes, I am fine. I, I'm okay. No ambulance, I'm okay. Just sleeping . . . Wow . . . I'm okay . . . You scared me."

Reverend Sounders persisted. "Are you alone? Is there anyone gone for help?"

Chrissy thought, *Is this safe? Should I say my husband has gone for help?* She finally admitted she was alone, hoping she could trust this so-called reverend.

Reverend Sounders called to her an offer of a ride to the next town and explained how he was just returning home from a visit with an aged friend who was quite ill.

Reluctantly, Chrissy accepted the offer, and she slowly moved to unlock the door of her car.

As Chrissy climbed from her car, the Reverend Sounders took her arm, helping her through the mud to the passenger door of his car. Starting off, he advised that they were about fifteen minutes from the town, and in the morning, he would call the local garage owner at home to have him pick up her car. Meanwhile, he further affirmed, he would drop her at the motel in town, and he told her to not worry about payment for the room—the owner was a friend and would not charge her, considering her misfortune.

As they drove, Chrissy's eyes stared out the passenger window while Reverend Sounders flooded the air with questions of where she was going, where she was from, and on and on.

All Chrissy was able to reply was her first name and that she was going to her aunt's place, stating that she was a bit dizzy from the accident and still quite sleepy.

She knew the aunt part was not true.

Through all the questions and all the time in the car, she avoided any eye contact with the reverend, all the while keeping one hand on the car door handle and the other on the seatbelt latch.

Having endured the longest fifteen-minute drive of her life, they finally pulled up in front of a quaint little eight-unit motel. It would appear that they had arrived in the Swiss Alps.

The motel was heavily laden with gingerbread wood-work. Each unit had its own dormer. In the moonlight there was what looked like animal carvings in each peak.

Reverend Sounders approached the main office and pushed a button beside the door. Within a couple minutes a woman opened the inner door and with a large smile greeted the reverend.

Chrissy could not hear the conversation, but the pointing to the car and the smiles and nodding led to the reverend walking back with a key to unit 3.

Grabbing the backpack that she had taken from her car, Chrissy walked with Reverend Sounders to the unit. He confirmed that for sure there would not be a charge for the room. After taking the key and thanking him, she unlocked the door. Entering, Chrissy switched on the light to a very clean, well-appointed, but small room.

Attaching the safety chain on the closed door, she dropped the backpack to the floor.

Stumbling forward while kicking off her shoes, she fell facedown across the bed, exhaling a sigh of relief and escape.

It was only a few seconds before she was sound asleep.

CHAPTER

The sunlight washed the room with warmth through the closed drapes as Chrissy woke.

Looking around, she pieced together the events of the previous day. The circumstances that demanded the sudden need to flee. The accident, Reverend Sounders, and how she got to the room. Even though the room was warm and the bed a well-needed comfort, she felt the best move she could think of was to get her car and get back on the road.

After having a quick shower and cleaning her shoes and clothes of dried mud, she grabbed her backpack and returned the key to the office.

The young boy at the office pointed Chrissy in the direction of the local garage as he explained that there was only one garage in town, and he wished her a wonderful day. The garage was only a couple blocks away.

The sun was warm, and the smell of spring hung in the air. But Chrissy barely noticed as she walked head down, only giving a shallow nod as people wished her a good morning.

As she approached the garage office, Chrissy heard a voice call out, "Good morning! Are you the lady that owns this car?" Looking in the open bay door, she saw a man in his forties beneath her car on the hoist.

She nodded.

"I'm Matthew. Everyone calls me M and M, you know, for Mat the Mechanic. You have quite a mess here," he explained as he grabbed handfuls of mud from the car's undercarriage. "I already see one wheel is turned in, and I won't know how much damage is done 'til this is all cleaned up. You may as well go over to Debbie's Diner 'til I know, and come back in about an hour and a half."

Chrissy turned and looked across the street and three doors down to see the diner. She didn't want to show her face around town, but as she had not eaten for a day, she felt she would grab something quick.

Entering the small diner, she was met with a smile and a warm greeting from a grandmother-looking waitress behind the counter. "Just grab a seat anywhere, honey," the waitress sang out.

Looking around, Chrissy chose a table in the back corner. The diner reminded her of what she saw in old movies. Six tables with bright red-and-white checker table-cloths were down the left wall. Each had bright-red leather benches. And centered on each table, against the wall, was a remote selector for the jukebox. The main jukebox itself was against the back wall between the tables and the counter.

The counter had approximately twelve chrome stools with red padded leather seats. It ran front to back to the right of where she stood in the entrance door. Behind the counter was a serving aisle and a mirrored wall with the soda fountain and milkshake machines flanking the kitchen pass-through.

There were only two elderly ladies, a middle-aged couple, and one other man in the restaurant. Although they all smiled and voiced a greeting, Chrissy kept her head down, returning the greeting with only a nod and an awkward smile as she passed where they sat.

Seated slammed against the wall as if to melt into the floral wallpaper and facing the door, she slouched low.

The waitress delivered a glass of water and a menu and started to recite, "Good morning, I'm Liz, and today's special—" to which Chrissy interjected, "May I please have a veggie omelet and tea with lemon?"

"Of course, honey," came the reply. "You must be the young lady the old reverend Sounders rescued last night. He was in here an hour ago and told us all about you. I'll get your order and be back in two shakes."

When first entering the diner and seeing the waitress, Chrissy had a feeling she knew her from somewhere. Her reasoning was that even though there was no resemblance, it must be that the waitress reminded her of her own grandmother. Her mother's mom and dad had both passed away by the time she was eight, and her dad's father a couple years later. Her dad's mother—Granny, as she called her—was someone very special in Chrissy's life.

A sweet, kind lady, Granny was always there, and with gentle words, she would solve any and all of Chrissy's problems while growing up.

After breakfast, Chrissy made her way back to the garage. She again was greeted by well wishers as she continued to keep her head down to avoid any eye-to-eye contact.

Approaching the garage, Chrissy found Matthew ankle-deep in mud, and those crisp blue coveralls he had on earlier now had a camouflage look. Lifting the safety goggles to his forehead, Matthew advised, "Part of your car's front steering is for sure damaged. New parts would need to be ordered, and they would take at least a day to arrive."

Feeling she had no other option, Chrissy agreed to the order.

After giving the approval, she made her way to the local general store. There she bought some sandals, a toothbrush and toothpaste, and some lighter clothes. Fearing a credit card would be too easy to trace, Chrissy paid with the limited cash she had on hand. Her sudden rush to escape left her no time to pack for a trip—a trip she did not know was coming.

Making her way back to the motel, she checked in for another night, thanked the lady in the office for their kindness, but said she would like to pay for both nights.

Barricading herself in the room and leaving all the curtains drawn, she threw herself on the bed to try and work out a plan—a plan for the situation she was now in. Not just with the car but all that the past twenty-four hours had brought.

Exhausted, she lay back on the bed and, fully dressed, drifted off to sleep.

CHAPTER

T he warm sun piercing the curtain's weave once again hailed Chrissy's start to the day.

The gentle warmth of the sun and a soft bed could almost make her want to enjoy another few hours sunk deep beneath the cozy blankets. But she knew that was not an option. She knew she had to be on the road, and as quickly as possible. That meant putting this town and a lot of miles behind her.

Chrissy showered and packed the few things just purchased in her backpack then listens to the morning news on the television. She was not sure what, if anything, may be on there, but she intently and nervously listened. Hearing nothing but local news and feeling there was still a safe passage, she left the motel for the garage and hoped her car was ready to go.

Arriving at the garage, she was greeted with a smiling Matthew, a.k.a. M and M. "Good morning. How was your sleep? Another fine day in our little part of the world—well, weatherwise. I just had a call from my parts supplier. One main part we need is not in stock, and they have to wait for an order to come in from the main depot. It should be here in two to three days. Sorry about that. This is a good chance for you to explore our wonderful little town."

A sudden chill ran up Chrissy's spine. She nervously bit her lip as she stared blankly into space.

"Are you all right?" Mat queries, noticing her blank stare and nervous reaction. "I could lend you my car if you needed to get somewhere local."

Chrissy, knowing that the farther the better was what was needed, replied, "Aw, thanks, but no thanks. I . . . I guess I will have to wait. Are you sure there is not another suppler for the parts or even used parts?"

Mat advised that he had tried all his sources. "Because your car is not even a year old yet, there are no used parts available. I will do everything possible to push things along for you."

As she walked away from the garage, Chrissy recalled the time she was learning to swim. She remembered how she was only eight feet from the cottage dock and felt something rub against her leg. That same feeling of panic was here again, as when with arms flailing, she struggled to stay above water and make it to the dock and get out of the water as quickly as possible.

Her pace quickened as she headed to the motel, hoping a room was still available. She just wanted to get behind a closed door and stay there until the garage called. Unit 3 seemed to be her sanctuary for what she hoped would be a very short stay in this town.

With curtains drawn, she sat cross-legged on the bed, staring at herself in the dresser mirror across the room. She thought of how, at only thirty-three years old, she should have her whole life ahead of her, but here she sat, scared and afraid of being noticed. With her natural blonde hair and her athletic figure, she was always noticed and proud of her appearance. Now she only wished that she could magically transform her image.

Combing her shoulder-length hair back with her fingers and pulling up her bangs, Chrissy attempted to create a completely different look. She thought maybe if she cut her hair and dyed it darker, she could alter her appearance enough to at least avoid recognition. Glancing to make sure the door was locked and chained, and the curtain tightly drawn, she grabbed her backpack and dumped the contents on the bed.

Along with the spring clothes, toothbrush, and toothpaste she had just bought came an avalanche of cash.

Pushing the clothes aside and scooping the bundles of bills in front of her, she began counting and piling. Stacking the cash in piles of $1,000, she determined that she had sixteen thousand dollars. Nervously glancing around, she neatly stacked the bills in the very bottom of the backpack. Chrissy grabbed the local Village Summer Events pamphlet from the nightstand. She placed it on top of the cash in an attempt at a false floor. She then piled her new clothes on top of that.

Keeping one hundred dollars aside for her pocket and tying her hair back, she got ready to go to the general store for scissors and hair dye.

After stuffing the backpack under the bed and hanging the "Do Not Disturb" on the outside of the door, Chrissy scanned the street.

Closing the door behind her, she started off again with head down and at a quick pace.

While Chrissy shuffled through the aisles of the general store, avoiding those with other shoppers, she was struck with a strange sensation that she had been here before—that déjà vu feeling. Not so much for the store itself, but the people.

She shrugged the feeling off as a strange coincidence or the fact that her own paranoia was starting to play games with her mind.

Along with the scissors and dye, Chrissy grabbed some clothes that she felt would work better with the new look—clothes that were a bit more funky than she would normally wear. Clothes she told her mother she would not be caught dead in.

Those memories ringing in her head sent a cold chill through Chrissy. *Dead!*

Back in her room, Chrissy stripped down and readied herself for the transformation.

* * *

She was pleased with her new black hair.

She then started cutting, leaving a jaw-length tail at the front on one side and trimmed closely on the other.

Having donned the new drab, baggy clothes and a head bandana, she stepped back to view the new her in the mirror.

"If mom could see me now," she whispered as a sad smile came across her face.

Cleaning her mess from the bathroom, she felt she had best get something to eat, and she called the front desk for a local pizza shop.

The female voice on the other end warmly admitted, "There isn't actually a pizza store in town." She advised, however, "The local diner does do a pretty good pizza, but they do not deliver. I can have my son run down and get it for you if you want."

Thinking she did not want anyone in or around her room, Chrissy replied, "No, that's fine. The walk will do me good. Thank you."

By this time the sun was starting to set.

Chrissy felt a little more comfortable with the new look and the darker time of day to venture out of the sanctity of her room.

The walk to the diner was the first inkling of any freedom Chrissy has felt for the past three days. Although still guarded, her gait was a bit more at ease, and she glanced up more at her surroundings. Whether this was because of the evening light or the new look or both, it did not matter. The feeling released some tension—for a short while anyway.

Arriving at the diner, that same grandmother image, Liz, greeted Chrissy with a warm welcome and the same "Sit any-where" smiling gesture.

Picking the same back table, Chrissy noticed quite a few more people were here this time, all still casting a welcoming smile to her as she passed their tables. Liz approached with the menu and a glass of water and started her introduction then suddenly stopped and blurted, "Hey . . . I know you!"

Chrissy felt the blood drain from her face and her whole body go cold.

"You're that little thing that was in here for the veggie omelet. Love your new look, honey."

As Chrissy's blood pressure slowly returned to normal, she thanked the waitress and asked about their pizzas.

Taking the pizza to go, Chrissy returned to her room, still questioning if her transformation was enough. As she sat cross-legged on the bed, eating, she thought about the people she had seen, not only in the general store and the waitress, but even the people she passed on the street and those in the restaurant. *Why do they all seem so familiar?* Again, was it only her paranoia, or had she seen them before?

The town itself did not look familiar, but maybe she had been here, or seen the people somewhere else. *Could it be that Dad drove through here on the way to and from the cottage?* She spent so much time with her head in her laptop then, only looking up once in a while. Maybe she remembered them from that time in her life. But that was so many years ago, and they still looked so familiar.

Chrissy wiped the thoughts from her mind as just a coincidence.

Stretching out on the bed, hugging one of the pillows as if it were a long-lost friend, she made a silent prayer for the car parts to come early as she faded.

CHAPTER

A knocking rattled Chrissy from her sleep, the first deep sleep she has had in a while. The knocking came again. It was someone at her room door. Blurry eyed, she rolled to look at the nightstand clock—8:23 a.m.

Being as silent as she could, she groped her way to the window and very slowly lifted the curtain from the wall, just enough to see toward the room door. She found herself looking at the back of a man standing there and speaking to someone down the walkway. She recognized the voice. It was Reverend Sounders. What did he want? Making her way to the door, she cracked it open, leaving the chain on.

"Yes," she muttered.

"Oh, I'm sorry. I must have the wrong room," Reverend Sounders blurted in surprise. Staring with a bewildered look, he then slowly questioned, "Miss Chrissy?"

"Yes," Chrissy replied, totally forgetting about her new look.

"I didn't recognize you at first. Sorry I must have woken you. I just wanted to check to make sure everything was all right with you. Liz from the diner told me you were still in town."

"Matthew from the garage happened to be there picking up his cowboy sandwich. Every day he has that same sandwich for breakfast, even for lunch as well sometimes! You know, that toasted western thing? He calls it a cowboy sandwich, though. I don't even think he has ever ridden a horse. Well, anyway, he did say that your parts should be in tomorrow, and your car will be ready by late afternoon."

"Great," Chrissy muttered with a cracking voice.

"So," Reverend Sounders continues, "our church annual spring bazaar is tomorrow morning, and I would be very pleased if you would join us. Liz makes some mean butter tarts, and some of our other ladies always bring a fabulous arrangement of sweets and sandwiches. Of course, there is always plenty of liquid refreshments. I make it *my* job to be the official taste tester. Don't want anybody going home with a sore tummy."

Chrissy projected a courteous smile as she listened to the kind Reverend's pitch, thinking that he perhaps had done a bit too much taste-testing.

The good reverend was about five feet six inches with a pleasantly rounded form, very rosy cheeks, and a highly polished dome surrounded by a moat of whitish-gray hair circling his head from ear to ear, reminding Chrissy of Friar Tuck from the Robin Hood book she loved so much as a child.

Remembering she was talking to him just through the cracked door, she excused herself for a moment and closed the door to remove the chain, and noticing she again slept in her clothes, opened the door shoulder-width. "That sounds lovely," Chrissy responded. "And thank you very much for thinking of me. I have a lot of planning still to do for when I get back on the road."

"Oh yes. Did you get a hold of your aunt to let her know what happened?" the reverend queried.

Chrissy stared blankly at the reverend then suddenly recalled the story she told him when they first met.

"Aw yes, yes, I did get a hold of her and she knows all about it and that I am safe," she blurted, hoping Reverend Sounders did not pick up on her dumbfounded expression.

Thanking the reverend again and excusing herself, she slowly closed the door, announcing that if she could fit it in, she would see him at the church tomorrow.

* * *

As far as Chrissy knew, she did not even have an aunt.

Her dad was the only son of a farming couple from the Midwest and spent his whole growing life there until he went to college in the East. That was where he met her mother, who was also an only child from a couple who ran a small garden center close to the college town. It was love at first sight for them. Her dad—a tall, dark-haired, and muscular farm boy with a bright wholesome complexion—drew a lot of looks from the girls. Those were not only for his handsome features but also for his kind mannerism and quiet brilliance. He, however, only had eyes for one girl—that shy strawber-ry-blonde beauty with the bright green eyes and the smile that could melt the polar ice caps.

Theirs was a match made in heaven. They dated throughout college and, in the second year after graduation, married. Within five years, they were the proud parents of two wonderful little children.

All of Chrissy's growing years seemed like a fairy tale. Her brother was the spitting image of her dad, and Chrissy was much like her mom but with blonde hair.

Harmony at home was something taken for granted. The love and understanding was just a way of life. Other than the odd scrap with her brother over bathroom rights, her growing up was something everyone would wish for, seemingly one you would only find in books. Her dad was a successful insurance broker, and her mom ran a small accounting business from home. They lived in a modest four-bedroom backsplit on a well-manicured lot.

The fairy-tale life, for Chrissy, seemed to have now crashed to an end. This princess was now staring into a broken mirror.

Chrissy has an overwhelming desire to call her mom, as she would do every Friday, just to check in. She knew this was something she should not do even though she knew her mom and dad worry when not hearing from her. Her reasoning was from thinking back to all the television mysteries she watched—there were always wire taps on the phones, and she did not dare to turn on her cell phone for fear of GPS tracking. Maybe it has not come to that yet, but she did not want to take a chance.

Thinking of Tommy, Chrissy wondered how life might have turned out if they had gotten together. As a young girl, this was a thought she had many times. That was until Ryan came along.

Tommy's parents owned a very successful manufacturing business. He was now heading the complete operation since his father took ill and passed away two years ago. Chrissy and he would still get together for lunch and laugh about old times at the cottage. Tommy has not had any really serious relationships. With the great success of the business, his big house, fancy cars, and large boat, he was a very eligible bachelor.

Ryan did not have any of that, but there was something about Ryan, something that drew Chrissy to him. No question, he was good-looking and smart, but there was a little magic that Chrissy could not put her finger on. There was that something that drew her to him.

Maybe she just knew Tommy too well, and Ryan was still a mystery for her to figure out—a mystery, she now wonders, that maybe she should have left unsolved.

CHAPTER

6

After grabbing something to eat at the diner, Chrissy's day was spent dashing about the small town picking up items she had listed that morning. Items to make herself ready for the road trip tomorrow.

Even though the days were now warming nicely, the evenings were still quite cool. On the list was a sleeping bag (should she again be caught having to sleep in the car), a case of bottled water, fresh fruit, and an assortment of candy and protein bars. Oh yes—and a slab of chocolate almond fudge, just to satisfy her sweet-tooth urges.

Back at her room, while packing her purchases of the day, she wondered why Liz was not at the diner this morning. The young girl there was very nice and an attentive waitress. For some strange reason though, Chrissy felt a sense of loss with not seeing Liz. It was strange that even though she did not want to be recognized, that same sense of fear she had was strangely there with not seeing Liz. This concerned Chrissy, and with her analytical mind, she tried to wrap a reasonable solution into the feelings.

The not wanting to be recognized was, in her mind, a simple one for the current situation she had now found herself in and the fact of not knowing if there was someone tracking her every move. This odd feeling she had when she did not see Liz—almost a panicked feeling—hit her as being very strange. Could it be that she now felt that Liz was a safe haven, and she would be grouped by Liz in with the locals at this point and not stared at questioningly? Another thought came to Chrissy. Could it be that Liz reminded her of Granny and that she always felt safe in her company and knew Granny could make everything turn out fine?

Chrissy rationalized that Liz was home making her signature butter tarts for tomorrow's bazaar. But still, silently, she hoped she would see her before she left town. The sweet butter tart thought sounded good.

Chrissy recalled the day she arrived home from school early and hungry. She rummaged through the pantry for some junk food, noticing in the back, behind boxes of cereal, was a fancy box of chocolates. Thinking as they must have been forgotten, they where fair game, she opened the box and allowed her sweet tooth to rule her willpower. She had attacked most of the top layer when Granny walked into the family room.

"You look like you have almost finished yours already," she voiced. "I haven't even opened mine yet." Granny wished Chrissy a happy Valentine's Day as she handed her a card.

After Grandpa's death, Granny had moved into the spare room next to Chrissy's. Earlier that morning, Chrissy's Dad had left a box of the same chocolates on Granny's pillow while she was downstairs making her morning tea.

She had forgotten totally that it was Valentine's Day and realized that these chocolates were probably meant for her mom. Evidence in hand, Chrissy ran to her room and stuffed the box of half-eaten chocolates under her bed.

After a half hour considering her excuse to her father for the missing chocolates, Chrissy returned downstairs in time to see her mom unpacking groceries in the kitchen. She was preparing to create another one of her wonderful meals, this one even more special, for her contribution to the Valentine spirit as she did each year.

Chrissy gave her mom a hug, and sat at the kitchen table while in her mind, rehearsing her explanation to her dad about how someone may have broken in and taken the chocolates and she thought she had seen someone going out the patio door as she arrived home from school. At ten years old, this was the best she could think of.

Chrissy recalled how, when Dad came home and before she got up the nerve to say anything, he, after dinner, went to the pantry and returned, presenting *the* box of chocolates to Mom and gift baskets of chocolate hearts and candy kisses for her and Brad.

With mouth wide open, she sat staring, dumbfounded, at the box. Seeing it had not been opened, she switched her questioning stare to Granny, who just sat there quietly with a big loving smile looking back at her.

Oh, how she wished Granny was still around to help her now!

Chrissy spent the day surfing the limited television channels available for any news related to her or broadcast of a police search or manhunt, all the while forming mental notes of what the last three days have brought into and taken from her life. This included possible ways to correct or solve the pending issues. Looking at her situation from all angles, she felt at this point the only route was an escape route. At least until she had further information to find a way to go home again.

This was the first time in Chrissy's life that she did not have the input from any of her family, or even Tommy. At this point though, she did not know how to tell any one of them the trouble she was in or how serious it was. She still did not know herself how serious it was to become.

It was now early evening, and Chrissy called the diner to order the same veggie pizza. This time, she decided to have Kenny, the motel owner's son, pick it up. She was not in the mood to face anybody from the diner at this time.

The escape route tomorrow was going to be enough exposure. Tonight's plan was to be packed and ready to go and have a good sleep for a long drive tomorrow. *Good sleep?* she questioned. It was something that had been a rare commodity of late.

CHAPTER

C hrissy again woke to the warmth of the sun flooding the room. With the sun backdrop, the floral pattern on the drapes seemed to be more vibrant this morning than she recalled. For some reason, all seemed clearer today. Possibly it was a relief response to knowing she would be back on the road and finally leaving this town. Strange, though, how that also left a little bit of a sadness with her. This unwanted stay may have become some sort of a cave for her to hide in.

This thought evoked memories of how, as a child, she would tent her blankets off the bed posts. That then would create a cave area that she and her favorite little bear, Mr. Ming, would play in. Why she called him Mr. Ming, she had no idea, but she and he felt safe in there.

She thought that it didn't matter how safe she was becoming with this little town and all the seemingly kind people in it. Those people that she oddly felt she knew, had met, or strongly reminded her of someone. In itself, that part of the comfort was so strange.

Well, she thought, *time to go.*

Chrissy readied to head off to the diner for her veggie omelet. Then, she thought, to the garage to check on her car and pick-up a map to see exactly where she was and where to go.

Opening her room door and full face into the warm morning sun, she was confronted with a beehive of activity. People walking, talking, shopping. It is as if the town had erupted with human forms. *Oh,* she reasons, *Saturday morning and the church bazaar, and maybe just the beautiful spring day.*

The thought seemed so unguarded. It was something strange to Chrissy for the last week. Maybe she was letting her guard down—not good!

Chrissy quickly looked back into the room to make sure the backpack was not left out then glanced at the outer door handle to confirm the "Do Not Disturb" was still in place—something that had become a permanent fixture. All good, she put her hands up to the side of her head. She was not sure why. This impulse reaction might have been to confirm her hair was short and she was still incognito.

Eyes focused on the sidewalk and with her head lowered, she set off.

The warmth of the sun, the sound of people talking, the smell of new mowed grass, and birds singing praise to the day—these were all familiar and a total recall of why she loved this time of year best. And just for all those reasons, it was like life renewed in so many ways—for them, at least. Would it ever happen for her again? The thought brought a sadness to her when she was only starting to feel a glimmer of joy, even if only a guarded joy.

The walk to the diner drew many more well wishes for a good morning, wishes that Chrissy now responded not with just her nod and reluctant smile, but a muttered "Good morning" as well.

Entering the diner, she found every available seat taken. The table she would call hers was occupied by two elderly ladies in bright floral-print dresses and large brimmed hats that would appear to be their garden plots.

Their cackle could be heard throughout the small diner, but no one seemed to mind.

In fact, they all seemed to be a part of it, as if they were all one big family. This might be what it was like in small towns—like at the cottage.

Chrissy recalled the night campfires. It did not matter which cottage the fire was at, people came and went all night like family dropping in.

Just then, a couple that were sitting at the counter got up to leave. Even though she would feel she was in a fishbowl, it would seem to be her only option. Sitting, she found herself beside a distinguished-looking gentleman on her left.

He was dressed in a dark-blue pinstriped suit. A blue silk ascot blossomed from his crisp white shirt, which complemented his full head of pure white hair. His total persona gave the impression that he came right off an old Hollywood movie set. He was a very wholesome-looking and very handsome older man.

From her seated position, the mirror behind the milkshake machine and to the right of the pass-through gave her a view of about three quarters of the patrons. *Not such a bad spot,* she thought. She could check them out without seeming to stare.

What she saw was a group of people that all had smiles and comforting words. Patting the shoulder of each seated patrons, they came or went offering warm gestures.

This was very strange to Chrissy, considering her past few days. Her life had now changed so much. For Chrissy, the old world she had just run from was unfolding as she thought it should—with what she thought at the time to be a mutually good relationship and money influx more than she expected. Then one turn of a page made it all look so different.

While finishing her omelet, she listened to the movie star, who turned out to be a retired Navy admiral. He was a very interesting, soft-spoken man, with a clear and concise way about him. She felt that had she known him better and could confide in him, he would be the type of clear-minded person she could depend on to help her through this life-changing issue.

As Chrissy left the diner and walked to the garage, it dawned on her how the admiral was a mixture of her father and his father (Grandpa).

While walking, she allowed her vision to steal quick looks at the town. She recognized how small it really was. The whole town seemed to be set on the one main street. From the diner, she could see straight through to the other end. At the far end, you could see the church set on a small hill just past the road that bent to the left in front of it. This made the church look like the road stopped there.

Chrissy could clearly see a large group of people at the church for the bazaar. Any thought that Chrissy had to possibly drop by in hopes to see Liz was now gone, considering the amount of people she would be swimming with.

Entering the lot of the garage, she could hear the ratcheting of an air powered tool and the purr of a compressor. Through the open bay door, Chrissy saw that her car was being worked on, which gave her some glimmer of hope to be back on the road.

Matthew called out a warm good morning and the reassurance that the parts were all there and her car is on track for completion. He confirms that by three o'clock her "little girl," as he called it, would be ready to go.

This brought a genuine smile to Chrissy's face. Gesturing toward the office, she asked if he had a map of the area.

Matthew, grabbing a rag and wringing his hands while screwing his face up in that "Oh my gosh, I forgot" look, advised that he was so sorry, but the last one went last week, and he had not ordered any yet.

Chrissy's smile quickly went to a look of concern. It was bad enough being stranded here. At least there was a town. The area seemed remote, and she feared how far it may be to another town. Chrissy wanted to ask questions on directions but hesitated. She was afraid that someone could come by asking about her. She would rather the townspeople had no answers to give.

Letting Matthew know she would see him at three, she turned to make her way back to the motel, this time paying more attention to her surroundings.

As she had already noticed, the town seemed like a one-main-street town. This, from what she could see, was the only street. Other than the commercial buildings aligning this main street, she did not see any residential properties. Behind the storefront properties, looked to be only forest. There must be a subdivision further down the road that she would most likely pass on her way out of town.

Going straight to the motel office, she checked out and advised that she would be leaving her room at two forty-five.

Back at unit 3, she left the "Do Not Disturb" on the door and turned on the news as she did a very thorough search of the room to make sure there was no evidence of her being there. Sitting on the edge of the bed, she stared at the new her in the mirror, recognizing a very big change from the Chrissy she knew and was so proud to be. She suddenly thought of the car. Not that it would almost be ready, but that it was still her car.

She had not even thought of that. The license plates, the make, the model, and the color would all be a huge giveaway. She was going around with a flag saying, "Hey, I do not look like Chrissy, *but I am*! Just check the flag I'm driving!" Maybe she should have left the car in the ditch and found something else to drive. Although at that point, she did not know how much money she had.

She was surprised to find that much was in the backpack. Ryan had said that if she were out and ever needed some cash, he had put some in a backpack under the carpeted panel over the spare tire. She had thought possibly one to two hundred. Finding that much was an even more cause for concern. Still, it was not enough to buy another reliable car. If she traded her car for another one, there would be a record of sale, and they would even have the record of the new car that she traded for.

The other option is to change the number plate. But how would she do that? She would have to steal a set off another car. *Well,* she thought, *just another few years added to the sentence.*

She sat forward with her face in her hands, her right leg shaking as she tapped her heel up and down on the floor— something she would do when she was extremely nervous. *Why not go all the way?* she thought.

Maybe there was a farmer in this area who would trade an old pickup for her new high-end BMW. That suspicious move would not just be a flag, but a whole damn load of fire-works signaling HERE SHE IS!

Okay, she thought, *calm down, there must be something I can do. I don't even know if there is a search party or posse out for me, or whatever it would be.* There was still no mention of anything on the news to cause concern. *So,* she reasoned, *just get the car and move on.*

Turning to glance at the clock on the nightstand, she saw it was two forty-three. Climbing into the backpack and doing one more visual sweep of the room, she set the key on the nightstand, put the "DO NOT DISTURB" on the inside handle, and set off to the garage.

CHAPTER

8

Chrissy's walk to the garage was showing signs of a lighter attitude with the anticipation of her car being ready to go.

She had walked for about one block and was at the point that she could just start to see the garage building when someone's voice called out from behind her, "Chrissy?" She did not know whether to turn or pick up the pace. The voice did sound familiar. Stopping to turn, she saw an elderly lady. The lady was wearing a beautiful, soft rose-colored dress that was flowing with her lively pace. Her bent arms were swinging like an Army sergeant's as she stepped quickly toward Chrissy. It was Liz.

Chrissy at first did not recognize Liz, she was so used to seeing her in her powder-blue diner's dress with the white collar and cuffs and those white nurse's shoes. "Wow," Chrissy commented in amazement as Liz approached, "you look fantastic."

"Oh, this old thing?" Liz replies with a big smirk as she grabbed Chrissy and delivered a kiss on the cheek and a big hug. "Sold all my tarts," she boasts, "and made some money for the church. Not sure how that happened though, with the old rev's paws in there. I let him have a few then had to smack his hand after about six or eight of them. Told him he'd ruin his figure." Liz chirped out a laugh with her fists on her hips in an "I told you so" stance. "I was hopin' I would get to see ya before you left. Are you all packed up and ready?" Liz took Chrissy's arm in hers and walked her to the garage. There they found the car already outside, all washed up and looking ready.

Matthew (M 'and' M) called out from the open garage door, "Miss Chrissy, it's all road-tested, filled with gas, and ready to go."

Liz gave Chrissy another hug and kiss as she told Matthew to "treat this girl right, ya hear?" Then, whispering in Chrissy's ear, she said, "He's a good, honest boy. Take care, honey. You come back, OK? Gotta give the diner the tart news. Bye."

After thanking and paying M and M (Matthew), Chrissy got into her car to leave, but for a few minutes, she just idled at the edge of the garage lot by the road, looking at the diner, before driving off. She felt like she was losing her granny all over again. Chrissy felt secure and insecure at the same time—happy to have her car and be on the road, but sad that she *had* to be on the road.

As a child, if Mom and Dad were upset with her, they would send her to her room as a punishment. This was the worst punishment for her. She was always a social butterfly, and to be banished to what she called "the dungeon" was life-ending. No phone, no laptop, no television. The world was going to end while she was in there, and they would forget about her and she would be caught in the lava flow. Even though there was not a volcano for hundreds of miles, the lava would make it to her room. Or maybe a tsunami would come and drown her as she sat on her bed while the water rose and she was not allowed to leave her room. The house was two thousand miles from the ocean, but she knew it could make it to her room. She was only on the second floor.

All these thoughts she recalled, and how she wished that she were back in her room, that safe haven. A tsunami sounded better than what was going on now.

CHAPTER

As she left town, Chrissy had checked the built-in car compass and confirmed she was heading south. The GPS did its search for a satellite connection and had done so several times over the last couple hours. She did hear Kenny and his mom talking to another person at the motel and saying the nearest town was 265 miles away. What she did not get was if it was south or north. No map, no satellite. What next?

She thought 265 miles meant she would be there in about another 3½ hours, and the sun was already cresting the tree line along the road. Driving at night was never in Chrissy's list of comforts. She had always been a car-top-down, sunshine kinda girl.

She thought about her first car. It was a secondhand Mustang convertible—no big motor or snappy sound, just a cool cherry-red Mustang with some nice wheels. She thought it was the perfect fit for her. During the first summer she had it, she would drive to the cottage alone, top down, hair blowing in the wind. Let Mom and Dad take Brad in the four-door family sedan. That did not suit the image she wanted at eighteen years old, a full-grown woman now, she thought.

She must have washed it every day for that first summer. Her dad would say how she was going to wash the paint right off the metal soon.

Even though it was used, it was new to her, and she was very proud of it. She saved every penny from her babysitting and working at the drugstore. Her mom would also have her help with her accounting business. Maybe that was why she now does—well, did—bookkeeping and is—or was—working on her accountant degree.

The sun is now fully behind the trees, and she still had two hours to go. That was if she was going in the right direction. Chrissy saw a road sign coming into view. Maybe this was the town sign. As she came within reading distance, she saw that it identified a roadside stop area with washrooms coming up in two miles. She didn't know if she was heading in the right direction or even if there was a gas station coming up. And if there was one ahead, would it be open?

The rest stop was her best bet for safety because of the bright lights, and there usually were trucks there, should she feel threatened. After all, she did prepare with a warm sleeping bag.

Chrissy pulled into the rest stop and found a good spot between two lampposts. From this location, she was in a shaded area yet had a lighted visual of the surrounding parking area. This left her with some sense of security.

There were only two trucks in the rest area, and the road was not busy, maybe because it was a Saturday night and everyone was home with their family. The only sound she heard through the partially open window were some frogs croaking in the distance and a cricket singing its lullaby. How she loved hearing that at the cottage on a warm summer night. The cherry on top would be the haunting call of a loon at a distance. Sweet music!

Before she shut the car off, Chrissy did another check of the GPS—still no satellite service. She reclined the seat and grabbed the sleeping bag, dragging it over her as she watched the last ray of sun as it vanished from between the trees. Checking the door locks and leaving the window down only a crack, she closed her eyes to Jiminy's lullaby.

CHAPTER

⊰{ 10 }⊱

The early dawn calm was shattered with the sudden clatter of diesel engines.

The sun was barely peeking through the trees on the far side of the road. The cool fresh morning air hung heavy with the smell of damp pine needles. Close at hand Chrissy could hear birds chirping and singing their praise to the day. Echoing at a distance in the dense bush next to the rest area could be heard a single crow calling out a warning to its family.

Strange, but this had been the best night's sleep she has had in a while. Maybe the smells and sounds reminded her of the cottage so much that a security sensor was triggered in her brain. "Can use more of those," she muses.

Starting her car, she quickly checked the radio for news and tried the GPS again—early morning Bible hour and no GPS.

Thinking of the GPS reminded Chrissy of the time her parents rented a motor home. The idea was, before the kids got too independent to travel with their mommy and daddy, they would all take a trip to the East Coast. Dad, who fancied himself as a photographer, loved nature photos, with the ocean and lighthouses being his passion.

This mobile house had a GPS, but it was an early system. Dad used it for the first three days, and those days were the most memorable of the trip, at least for Chrissy and her brother. Still to this day, if they make a wrong turn they would look at each other and say "Recalculating."

At one point, the system had them going down a laneway that ended up to be a dead end. Dad had a car in tow for touring when in campgrounds, so he could not back up. The only solution was to drive through a lady's garden and squeeze the thirty-two-foot monster plus the added car between her house and a fence that left about one inch of clearance on each side. The lady was very nice about it, saying it was a good thing she got her carrots and beans out the day before.

Another time on the same trip, the GPS told them a route that must have been for mountain bikers, not the condo on wheels. The route was fine to start then went to a one-lane road. They had to stop four times to cool the smoking brakes down on the descent. That was only after they reached the crest of the mountain, crashing along at about one mile an hour. The tension between Mom and Dad was so thick it could be spread on toast. The nice part about that experience was that it showed that true love can shine through, because Mom and Dad are still together. After that experience, Mom locked the GPS in the glove box, and at the first gas station bought an *M-A-P*. The whale watching and the ocean were great, but the trip there was for sure the most memorable.

"Time to move on," Chrissy muttered. The early spring air was crisp and refreshing on the dash to and from the rest area washroom to brush her teeth and have a quick wash.

Packing away the sleeping bag, she restarted the car for some warmth then grabbed a protein bar and a bottle of water.

Heading out again, Chrissy noticed the lack of traffic, and hopes the next fuel stop is not too far. In fact, this morning, she has not seen any traffic at all, which was strange but nice. She was still very guarded, and the lack of traffic meant she was invisible.

Maybe she should have been that way years ago when she first met Ryan. She wanted to be noticed by him right from the first meeting, although she was unaware of that at the time. She thought the feelings she felt as a teenager were shallower then they really were. The guy was cute, seemed to be smart, and was very quiet. She thought it was only curiosity that drew her to him. Now in a different light and with clarity of mind, she realized that what she wanted to do was to solve the Ryan mystery at whatever the cost—a cost that she now realized was far greater than she ever thought it could be.

Her life with Ryan started the very first day the family returned from the cottage. She would not admit it then, but now she saw that was the start.

That whole summer, she would find excuses for a reason to talk to him. He was always there but did not seem to be that interested in her. This made the quest even more demanding for her. She would do things like bake a cake and take some to him with the cover story that she made it for Dad and they could not eat it all. After all, Granny always said that the way to a man's heart was through his stomach.

She would loosely praise his accomplishments and appear to be aloof when he asked her something, like the time he got his driver's license and later bought a small motorcycle. He was so proud of that bike, and when he asked if she wanted to go for a ride, she pretended it was not such a big deal. Inside, her heart was about to jump out of her body.

The game was to make him want and notice her.

Well, it worked. And maybe too well.

They started dating when she was sixteen, and all seemed to be going fine. She always had the feeling, though, that he was holding something back. This was maybe why she hung on for so long—there was still a mystery to solve.

Throughout high school their relationship was an on again and off again one. Not that they dated anyone else. There just seemed to be a lot of cooling-off periods. Looking back, it would now appear that neither one wanted the relationship to be too serious.

After high school, Chrissy followed in her mother's footsteps and secured a position with an accounting firm. The plan was to work toward her CPA degree. Her dream was to one day open her own practice and specialize in forensic accounting. She thought it would be the perfect career for her, allowing her fair and analytical mind to work investigating, assessing, then commenting on professional negligence claims.

Forensic accountants also engaged in marital and family law. They analyzed lifestyles for spousal support purposes, determining income available for child support and equitable distribution. She had heard so many cases of an unfair balance in that area and felt she could make a fair and recognizable difference. And like a Dick Tracy of the accounting world, she would be involved with situations relating to criminal matters that typically arise in the aftermath of fraud. Granny always called her Dick Tracy's little sister (Chrissy had to google who he was).

This, to Chrissy, was all very exciting.

Fuel was getting low, and there was still no sign of a town or even a gas station. Commenting to herself, Chrissy questioned why this whole area seemed to be an area she had driven through or seen before. Again, it might have be an area that Dad drove through on the trips to the cottage. These thoughts were still hanging as she passed an area where the shoulder was dug up for a good two hundred feet. She thought someone else had the same misfortune as herself, it would appear—possibly another wild animal incident.

Driving on, she recalled her mishap and her hero, Reverend Sounders. She considered everything now—the town she was stranded in, all the people that seemed so familiar, and now the road itself was also looking so familiar. So she concluded this, for sure, was a route that her dad had taken as part of the trip to and from the summer cabin. That was a clear explanation for the recognizable people and places.

The sun was shining, the road was clear, and Chrissy was feeling good about moving on. Her mind was racing though. Where is she moving on to?

It was now 2:36 p.m. Still no GPS—bad news. But there were still no helicopters, roadblocks, or news on the radio. That so far was good news. Her concern now was the fuel.

Rounding a bend in the road, she saw buildings through the trees as the road seemed to bend again to the right up ahead. At last, there should be a gas station there. As she reached the other bend, she saw a church on the left—a church that was all too familiar.

She was back where she started from!

How did this happen? She did not recall making turns off the main road. When she got back on the road this morning she could not have gone the wrong way because she was now coming in on the north of town. If she had left the rest area going in the other direction, she would be coming back into town on the south, the same area she just left from yesterday.

Now she realized why that portion of the road with the shoulder all dug up was so familiar: it was her dug-out mud slide!

Totally confused, she pulled over to the side of the road to run back over her moves in her mind. The frustration of the past week was bad enough, but to travel almost two days and be where she started from, she could not comprehend. The best move, she felt was to head to Matthew's, fill the car up, drop in at the diner, and have something other than the protein bar and water. *But first, see if unit 3 is available.*

Chrissy stopped at the motel, and her sanctuary was ready and waiting. She then headed to the garage, which was closed. She had forgotten it was Sunday. Well, a good meal and the thought of seeing Liz was a small comfort at this time of frustration.

The maple-glazed rainbow trout dinner was what she needed as a temporary fix to take her mind, for a short while, off her seemingly endless saga. She was, however, sorry that it was Liz's day off.

Heading to unit 3, Chrissy set plans for an early bed and early rise to make her escape. She was trying so hard to get to get to sleep, but this seemed futile. She spent most of the night tossing and turning. Her mind was just buzzing with the driving moves she made. No matter how much, or from what angle, she looked at it, she could not see how she got so turned around to end up right back where she started.

She had done that with Brad at the cottage. They would go walking in the forest behind the cottage each fall to pick pinecones and pretty, bright-colored leaves for the table arrangement for Thanksgiving. There were times she found herself guiding them in a circle. But this was a road, not a forest with no paths!

CHAPTER

❧{ 11 }❧

The warmth of the sun again was welcoming her to the day.

Chrissy woke with the strong urge to get to the diner to see Liz. With her unsettling night, her only thought right now was that a friendly face may help her to see things clearer. Hurrying to prepare to leave, she packed everything in her backpack and set off to the diner.

Her angst was slightly settled with the sight of Liz through the glass door as she approached the diner. As she stepped inside, Liz turned toward the opening door and, at the sight of Chrissy, burst out "Chrissy!" with an ear-to-ear smile. This seemed to cast out most of Chrissy's self-doubt feelings.

Liz swept her two arms across to point at the back table, saying "Your table awaits, madam." Chrissy cast a large smile, a smile that had been mostly guarded of late. Meeting Chrissy at the table, Liz took Chrissy's hand as she sat and held it in her two hands and softly said, "I've missed you, girl. I know it's just a couple days, but I still missed you."

Chrissy felt the tears well up as she murmured, "And me you."

"Veggie omelet coming up, OK, honey?"

Chrissy nodded, feeling she could not speak for crying. It was a busy morning at the diner, and Liz was bouncing back and forth from calling out orders at the pass-through to serving patrons. Chrissy had never really followed Liz as she worked. She had always kept her head down. She saw how Liz was a ray of sunshine to everyone that came in, whether she knew them or not. Wanting and hoping to talk to Liz would be impossible, she thought. Finishing her breakfast, she decided to just get back on the road as she slowly got up to leave.

Liz motioned her to wait as she finished with an order. Approaching Chrissy, Liz asked her to come back at four thirty, stating she would like to talk to her. Even though Chrissy wanted to leave as quickly as possible, she felt this was something she needed to do.

"See you then," Chrissy replies.

Heading back to the room, Chrissy decided to stay one more night and spent the day anxiously waiting for four thirty.

* * *

A sense of excitement flowed through Chrissy as she made her way to the diner. Although she knew she should be miles away at this time of day, she had a overwhelming urge to see Liz.

At the diner, Liz was just going over some call-in orders with that young waitress, the one whom Chrissy had met before. Liz greeted Chrissy and suggested they each take tea to go and walk to the park. Chrissy had no idea there was a park but said that sounded great. The sun was still quite high and the day was beautifully warm.

Liz took Chrissy's arm, and slowly they made their way to the park near the center of town. There was a walkway between two shops that led to a clearing in the forest. In the clearing was a beautifully manicured parkette. Sitting across from Chrissy at a picnic table, Liz took her hands as she asked Chrissy, "Tell me all about it. I knew from the first time I saw you, you had a weight twice the size of you that you were carrying. Then you made that change from the pretty little thing to the still pretty but totally different person. All the time it was obvious you did not want to be noticed."

Chrissy was shocked that it was so obvious. "What do you mean?" she blurted in astonishment.

"Well," Liz says, "We all have things in our lives that we would like to have turn out different."

Chrissy responded, "But, Liz, your life seems so perfect. You seem to enjoy your job, everyone knows you, and you know everyone. You call them all by name. The town seems so friendly, and since I have been here, everything seems perfect."

"Well, honey," Liz softly explains, "the happiest of people do not always have every thing they desire. They just make the best of everything they have. Life for me has not been a fairytale. But it was my life, and I remember all the good. Let me tell you a story.

"I was brought up by the most loving, understanding, and kind person you would ever want to meet. And considering her start in life, you would wonder how this could be. My Gran was the illegitimate child of a lady in England during the depression in the 1800s. At six years old, she was sold and shipped to Canada as part of the Home Children

Program along with hundreds of other children. She was a lowly domestic servant, like a real-life Cinderella.

"Eventually she saved her pennies and was able to leave and moved to the Niagara region of Ontario and worked as a picker on a fruit farm. That was where she met the love of her life. He was a migrant worker from Michigan. Eventually they married and had two wonderful children.

"One was my mom, and the other my uncle Solomon. Uncle Solomon unfortunately died of pneumonia when he was nine years old. My mom, Lillian, met and married my dad, Arthur, and had two children as well.

"Now, my brother was born with some serious issues that he continually had to visit the hospital about. I am not sure exactly what it was. That was never talked about. But on one of the trips to the hospital—I was five years old at the time and left with Gran—well, on the way, a gravel truck lost control and rolled over onto my parents' car.

"From that point on, I was raised by Gran. You know, Chrissy, never once in my life had I heard Gran complain about anything. She taught me that everyone has a problem. Some worse, some not so. But to each person, theirs is the most terrible thing. It is not our place to judge anyone else. We must love and respect each other.

"Gran taught me to make the most of what you have. She was thankful she was shipped to America, because she met my grandad and had many wonderful years with him. She was thankful for the time she had with the children she loved so much. She loved them both. She was thankful for the time she had with uncle Solomon. She was thankful to see my momma grow strong and healthy and marry a wonderful man, my dad. She was thankful she had me in her life.

And she told me every day. She also taught me to remember the times I had with my mom and dad and little brother.

"I am blessed that I had Gran in my life to love me and guide me. Believe it or not, she still guides me. She has been gone a long time, but when there are times in my life that are tough—and there have been—I would think of Gran and ask myself, 'What would Gran say or do?' The right answer is always there.

"Something else Gran always told me—'Don't push the river.' When she first said that, I thought she was joking. Then she explained, if you jump in the river and try to swim upstream, even though it looks smooth, there is still a current. Although your movement forward may be there, you work harder to achieve those gains and you get there slower. So if you turn around and flow with it, you gain ground faster and get to a place where you can rest sooner.

"'Lizzy'—that's what she called me, Lizzy—'life is like the river. Sometimes it is best to swallow your pride and move on. In the end you get where you want to go and make it there with much less effort.

"Chrissy, there must be someone in your life like my Gran that you can lean on now to help. All you have to do is sit back, think of times with that person, and hear that solution.

"Now some times the solution is not what you thought it might be. That does not mean it is not the right one for you. The point is that you move forward with a positive, rather than drown in a negative. Also, remember that on that trip to that place you want to be, there may be bumps or bends. Don't give up.

"Let's say you have a destination in life. Like you have told me about your cottage that you and your family went to. Okay, the road to the cottage seemed straightforward enough. Partway there you are hit with a rough road with lots of potholes. Then there is a detour sign that takes you a totally different direction. Eventually you are back on track and heading in the right direction. You will make it to the cottage in the end.

"Think of your problems in life like that. Sometimes there will be rough spots, maybe even a detour or two. But in the end, if you keep that goal the target, you will get there. Never lose sight of the goal you set for your destination."

"Wow," Chrissy breathes and then says, "that is so insightful. You, and your Gran seemed to have such a wonderful relationship. Did you have any children? Oh sorry, am I being too personal?"

"No, honey, that is not too personal. It unfortunately was not to be in the cards for me. I was married to a wonderful man. We had fourteen great years together, but the family did not happen."

"May I ask what happened to your husband?" Chrissy asks timidly.

"He was an Army man and I lost him to a foreign land. They never found the body. I still pray for him to return."

"I am so sorry, Liz. I should not have pried."

"Not at all, Chrissy. We had so many wonderful years together. Anyway, if we had been blessed with a child and it were a girl. I would have wished her to have been just like you."

Chrissy's eyes welled with tears as she squeezed Liz's hand. "Well, Liz, I guess you are ready to retire at some point."

Liz replies, "Now that is another thing that is not in the cards. Not that I really want to anyway. I actually retired five years ago. I used to work at a mill—a knitting mill. Five years ago they retired me out. I took the first year and washed my clothes twice each day, checked the mail four times a day, and bought one apple at a time from the grocery store for a reason to get out the next day. Retirement is not for me. Even if it was, I could not afford it now anyway."

Chrissy queries, "Why? You must have an Army pension, and did that mill not have one?"

"Sure, there is an Army one, and yes, the mill had one as well. Herby—oh, that's my hubby—ha ha, that's funny. I never called him Herby, My Hubby, before. Well, Herby and I started planning a long time ago for retirement. We thought we would see the world together. Herby had seen quite a bit with the Army, but he wanted me on his arm the next time instead of a rifle. We had quite a bit of savings, but that is all history now."

"Oh my gosh, Liz, what happened?"

"Trust—that is what happened. Although I am still doing OK."

"Who did you trust, a friend or relative?" Chrissy queried.

"Neither, honey. A good-lookin' smooth-talkin' man. There are at least fifteen of us I know of that invested with him. There was a flyer in the diner on that noticeboard at the front door. Double your money in five years. I think the slogan was 'Watch Your Money Grow.'

"You know, as Gran said, if it seems too good to be true, then quite possibly it is. So we all went to listen to this fella anyway, just to see if maybe we could get some ideas and do something ourselves. The banks give you next to nothing, so a look and a listen shouldn't hurt. In short, he did say that sure we could do it ourselves. And he was a professional, and he would make sure our money went into the right hands. I guess the hands he was talkin' about were his hands. So all of my savings, a good chunk from Hazel's at the general store—you met her, right? Even Matt put all the money in that he had gotten from his mom's estate when she passed.

"In all there was fifteen of us at that meeting that joined the band. I had heard some others from around the area were also in. In total I suppose this young fella is livin' the life of Riley. That flyer title should have been 'Watch Your Money Go.'

"Norm, Hazel's husband, said this guy was like Superman. He left town with the money like a speeding bullet. I do feel sorry for him though."

"Why?" Chrissy queries.

"Well, it is too bad someone has to cheat others to get ahead. I always felt cheaters lived a life not trusting anyone. Because that is the way they feel the world is. And it is not. It is a wonderful place with wonderful people like you, Chrissy. That person is missing out on wonderful people like you."

Chrissy asks Liz if she has any idea what time it is. Looking up at the sun, Liz replies, "I would say about seven forty-six." She gave Chrissy a sly look out of the corner of her eye.

They both laughed and decided it was time to head home. Well, home for Liz and to the diner for a quick dinner for Chrissy.

Walking out to the main street, Liz gave Chrissy a long hug and commented how she hoped Chrissy would spend a few more days in town and how wonderful it was to have their talk. They headed off in opposite directions. Chrissy slowly made her way back to the motel to freshen up before going to the diner.

CHAPTER

12

At the diner she was greeted by that wonderfully bubbly young waitress.

Heading to her corner table, Chrissy was stopped by the lady she and Liz were talking of earlier. Hazel and her husband, Norm, were just about to place their order when she invited Chrissy to join them. Chrissy's reluctance showed, and Hazel continued, "If you are by yourself, that is, you are very welcome to join us."

Considering it rude to decline, Chrissy smiled and accepted. Hazel shifted herself toward the wall and, patting the red padded bench seat, invited Chrissy to "unload right here."

"We have not been formally introduced. I am Hazel, and this is the love of my life, my wonderful hubby, Norm. I've seen you at our store a few times, the general store, and Liz raves about you."

"Oh?" Chrissy questions.

"Just the good stuff." Hazel laughs. "Have you newly moved, or planning to move into the area?"

"No, I was just passing through. Well, I had a bit of an accident and was rescued by Reverend Sounders—" Chrissy responds.

"Yes, we know about the accident," Hazel injects. "The good reverend told us all about it. He said that he had rescued a fair maiden in distress last week. I think it was at the church bazaar he told us. You have made quite a transformation since then, he said. Not too sure what that meant though."

They went through their dinners with Chrissy politely listening to the saga of the store roof leaks, the almost fire, and a storm that they thought was going to blow the whole roof right off. In all, Hazel's attitude was fun and light. She would laugh at almost every event that Chrissy would have found to be nerve-racking. There was a great balance of Hazel's powerful outgoing attitude and her husband's quiet supportive nature. They seemed to be a perfect match.

Chrissy found them quite refreshing to spend time with. This left Chrissy a little concerned. She was afraid she was letting her guard down. As comfortable as it was with the reverend, Liz, and these new people, she felt she should hold back.

The evening went well for Chrissy, with the time spent with Liz and the surprise encounter with Hazel and Norm. As nice as it was, it seemed unsettling for her. She was not sure if this was too normal, if this made sense, she thought. She would spend hours at the cottage with the neighbors even as a young adult, just listening to their take on life and adventures that they encountered on that journey. She always felt comfortable in the company of an older person and listening to what had happened in their youth. Maybe that was because she spent a lot of time with her Granny, and even when Grandpa was alive, she marveled at what he had done in his life. He had been a paratrooper in the Second World War, and he recited to Chrissy his training. How she thought that to be so exciting! Later in life though, she realized it meant he was going to and did drop into an area of the world that was just waiting to use him for target practice.

This really hit home with her when she was eighteen. She felt that eighteen was still at the start of her life, and she had her whole life ahead of her. She was only just beginning to plan what her life was going to be. The thought was terrifying that her Grandpa, at that same age, had to live a life not knowing if there would be one to live every minute of every day. She knew Grandpa was in a much worse position than she was, but it was a position he never complained about or even mentioned.

Still, her plans for life were yanked out from under her by her failing to see the real world. She realized how her blindness—and the events directly relating to that blind state—has now lead to her life on the run.

* * *

Chrissy had a very restless night. Her mind could not move away from the thoughts of Tommy and their times together. She wondered how her life would be right now if they had gotten together.

From the time she was three when her parents bought the cottage, she recalled, Tommy's mom and hers would get together on Saturday mornings. She also recalled that at those gatherings her Dad and Tommy's dad would go fishing.

It seemed to go on for years that Mr. Morton (Tommy's dad) would be outside their cottage very early Saturday mornings, always with thermos in hand and pacing. Mr. Morton was a hyper type, very kind and always had a joke to tell. He would appear to have the energy of two men.

All those Saturdays went by, and Chrissy could not recall one fish fry. She was not even sure if the hooks ever broke the surface of the water. It was long suspected by the wives that it was just a one-upmanship: who had heard the best joke of the week.

Well, when the two mothers got together, Chrissy and Tommy would play in the sand at the lake's shore, building castles. As they grew, the castles turned to forts. Then they had their bicycle challenges.

Tommy was always very creative, and the times when they would draw or color, his work was amazing.

Chrissy loved to create, but hers was more to the fashion side. She recalled how she would use Tommy as a manikin. How patient he was as she would drape him in anything and everything she could find around the cottage, even old drapes her mom was about to throw out that she convinced her mom were perfect dress material.

Chrissy would even apply her mom's makeup to poor Tommy. She then, with a designer intro to her mom and Mrs. Morton, would proudly display her model. Tommy would always do the sashay walk, the spin, and the contrapposto stance. He was such a great sport. It seemed that no matter what befell him at Chrissy's hands, he was a ready and willing participant.

There were so many times Tommy fell victim to Chrissy's dreams and schemes, and she did not recall one complaint.

Chrissy recalled at her home in town, she use to ride her tricycle around the in-ground pool. How her Dad was so adamant to stay away from the edge that when it came time to teach her to swim, she would not go near the water. No matter how hard Mom or Dad tried to get her into the pool or the lake at the cottage, she held on to them so tight. She was surprised they did not faint from the lack of blood circulation. It was Tommy, with his patience and gentle coaching, who finally broke through the barrier that had been built up. He may have regretted it later, though, with all her cannonballs and water antics aimed at him.

Tommy had been a part of her life as long as she can remember and her best friend through the entire time. Even though they would picnic together and go to movies together, she had always thought of him as her best friend.

Once he wrote a poem. He said it was for his goldfish. Only many years later did it dawn on her that that poem was most likely meant for her. She loved the poem but kidded him endlessly. "For your goldfish? On a *scale* from one to ten, this is one slippery relationship."

She still remembered the poem. It had been permanently etched into her mind. Tommy had since written many more, but this was his first, as far as she knew, and it made her so proud of her dearest friend. It was still in her memory today. She recalled the words, but her image of him talking to a fishbowl still drew a smile. The poem was called "Love" and went

> Love is a sound so soft and sweet
> Love is the ground beneath my feet
> Love is that touch that makes me say
> I've never ever felt this way
> Love is the strength that helps me see
> The one so hidden deep in me
> The one I thought I never knew
> 'Til love has touched and gave me you
> Master Tommy Morton, Esquire

He would always say that last line after his recital.

Chrissy would always laugh and clap then cheer, yelling, "Excellent, Master Tommy Morton, Esquire!"

Maybe she was so blind to his feeling that he never asked for more than what was there, a wonderful friendship. Tommy was always a very shy and very creative person. Was she so caught up in the friendship she did not see what was possibly the best thing in her life was right there in front of her? Or, as with her previous thoughts, was there no challenge? Maybe her personality of Dick Tracy mannerisms sent her in the wrong direction. Ryan was a challenge that was not there with Tommy. Maybe in accounting this was good, but with matters of the heart, other senses needed to be listened to. Tommy left her feeling safe in the relationship, trusting of who and what he was, knowing where she stood in it, and a total knowing that he would be there to support. All these were foreign with Ryan.

Her mom had taught Chrissy about many things, but how to listen to your heart was not one of them. Had Chrissy only discovered that secret earlier, she most likely would not be lying on a bed in the middle of the night in a town she new nothing about.

Except that almost everyone she met left her with a strange feeling she had seen them before. They did not seem to know her though. So was it on the way to the cottage, or was there another explanation? She was believing less and less that the cottage-route scenario was the answer.

Whatever it was, she had to find a way to shut down her mind and get some sleep. Tomorrow she had to leave early to get as many miles behind her as possible.

CHAPTER

13

Morning came far too early for Chrissy. Her lack of sleep lately had become an unwanted way of life.

As was now a standard practice, her first move of the day was to switch on the news channel, hoping her name was nowhere to be mentioned. Hearing nothing, she was both relieved and concerned—relieved that it was not in any news context and concerned that there might be a news blackout. Again the thought of her car and the registration plates arose.

She felt her best plan was to get to the diner for something to eat. Hopefully after a hot meal and a cup of tea, her mind would be awake enough to answer these riddles.

At the diner, Chrissy was again greeted with Liz's welcoming smile. This time there was an even more welcoming gesture. A projection of deep affection was very obvious as she pointed Chrissy to her table. As she slowly wandered to the back of the restaurant, almost every customer in the diner was smiling and wishing a good morning. This made her feel so warm and accepted as a part of their community. Given different circumstances, she could find herself settling for an extended stay.

Nestling into her corner table, Chrissy was joined by Liz. She wore a smile—although it seemed like a sad smile.

"Are you leaving us today?" Liz asked.

"Yes, I really need to be on my way," Chrissy responded, also with sadness in her voice.

"We are all going to miss you so much, Chrissy!"

Just then, the doorbell rang out as another patron entered the diner. It was Reverend Sounders, smiling and waving to each table like a politician would. When he had Chrissy's table in his sight, a giddy laugh came over him like a baby as you tickled its tummy. He suddenly broke into a quick waddle down the aisle, almost knocking Liz over as she headed to place Chrissy's order. With eyes fixed and his arms outstretched, upon reaching the table, he flopped his form on the opposite bench and reached across to grab Chrissy's hands.

"Hi there, fair maiden," Reverend Sounders chirped with glee. "I am so happy to see you. I thought you had abandoned us for greener pastures. I saw Norm earlier outside his store. He was setting up the outdoor display. All the rakes and shovels and the gardening paraphernalia. He always does an outdoor display for each season, event, or holiday. Most of them are very interesting—almost like going to an art gallery. He does such a wonderful display.

"Anyway he told me a secret. He mentioned you joined Hazel and himself for dinner last night. Got me a little jealous, I have to say. So may I have the pleasure of buying you breakfast?"

"I welcome and would love your company, but you do not have to pay," Chrissy responded.

"Well," says the reverend, "I insist. Have you ordered? I'm going to try one of Matt's Cowboy Sandwiches. Never have tried one, and I hope it is something good for a diet. The missus says it is time for me to shed a few pounds. This is going to be a rough ride for me. Got a bit of a sweet tooth, especially for those pies and tarts that sweet Liz makes. My mouth is watering just talking about them. I can see by your trim form you don't have any bad habits."

Chrissy thought how lucky she was the reverend couldn't read minds.

The breakfast took much longer to get through than Chrissy would have wanted. The time with the reverend was fun and entertaining, though. She heard all about the church bazaar of the past week. He had a wonderful way of explaining his take on things, similar to his official taste-tester position—how the bazaar was so busy one year he had the overflow parking on the lawn, which was all fine until he had them parking in the flower bed, and how his wife threatened to clear a spot in there for him to sleep if he didn't move the cars out. He said he loved the outdoors, but he felt he better move them "'Cause she would miss me with her being in that house all alone."

As each person would arrive or leave the diner, they would acknowledge their table with a wave and a smile both for the reverend and Chrissy.

The feeling of being part of the community was comforting and tempting for her to linger, but Chrissy knew the best for her was to move on. Although she had no idea where she was or where she was going, movement was, in her mind, the only solution. At least until she had more of an idea what was, or where was, a safe place to be. She still had no idea if anyone was out there looking for her—a thought that left her worried for her parents and brother. At this point they must be wondering why she did not make her usual Friday call last week. She had missed twice before, so her mom may be at ease for another couple days. By then there should be a solution, or at least a direction for her to pursue.

Chrissy thanked Reverend Sounders for breakfast and the lovely time. She stated how she enjoyed the conversation so very much. She thought even though she barely got twelve words in, the reverend was a delight to listen to. She excused herself, and after giving Liz a heartfelt hug, she started to make her way back to the motel.

All the way to the motel, her thoughts were of her mom. Her mom seemed to have such a clear way of solving problems. It was as if she had someone she would call to get solutions to anything. Sometimes Chrissy was not happy with the solutions, but as she grew, she realized her mom's answers were the best for the situation. As her dad always said, "Listen to Mom. She knows what she's talking about. She, for sure, is not just a pretty face."

She once asked her mom how she got so smart. Her mom said she was not alone. She had help. When Chrissy was old enough to understand, her mom explained.

It was now time to put into practice what her mom had said. Entering unit 3, she flopped back on the bed and closed her eyes, and her mother's words flowed to her.

"If you have a problem or need an answer to something, simply do this. Find yourself a comfortable position." At home Chrissy found lying on her back on the lawn worked. The bed would do today.

Then her mom would say, "Imagine you are lying in a meadow covered with wildflowers. Smell the flowers. Feel the gentle breeze as you look up at the beautiful blue sky. Hear birds singing off in the distance. Now slowly, a rainbow starts to appear in that clear blue sky. It gets brighter and brighter until it is rich with color. Still lying, you can see yourself in the meadow, as if you were now a bird and looking down at yourself.

"From that point of view, you can also see both ends on the rainbow. One end is way across the meadow, near an old tree rich with green leaves. The other end of the rainbow is about three feet from you lying there. You see your arm stretch out, and your hand is almost touching a bright gold pot.

"As your hand lies there, palm up, something starts to flow out of the pot. It feels like a calming flow of warmth that moves up your arm. It then reaches your shoulder, then goes up your neck, and covers your head. You then feel that warm calm feeling over your entire body.

With this warmth, there comes a clarity of thought. All your questions now seem to have answers. All the answers seem to be coming faster and faster. All your thoughts are getting clearer and clearer. You have a sense of clarity that is bringing forth solutions to your questions. Allow them to flow freely.

"Be patient, relax, and continue to feel the gentle breeze and the smell of the sweet grasses and wildflowers. Your body feels so relaxed as still your thoughts come clearer. All you need to do now is move to that solution that this calm has brought forth.

"And, Chrissy," Mom would say, "there is a whole universe out there ready and listening to help you. All you have to do is ask."

The air was sweet with the smell of the wildflowers. The tall meadow grasses and wildflowers were waving gently in the warm breeze . . .

Then a sudden loud knocking crashed Chrissy back to a beige room and a three-light fan fixture set against a stippled ceiling.

The knocking came again. But this time it did not seem near as loud as when she was in the meadow.

Launching from the bed, she pulled the curtain to see Kenny, the motel owner's son.

Chrissy then opened the door. "Hi, Kenny, can I help you?"

"Good morning, ma'am."

Chrissy hated when he said that. She felt she needed another thirty years added before she was a *ma'am*.

"My mother was wondering if you were leaving today."

"Yes, thank you, Kenny. I am just packing up."

"OK, ma'am, you have a great and safe trip, and if you are in the area again, please honor us with another stay."

Chrissy just smiled politely, and closing the door, she thought of how nice the mom and Kenny were, but she wished he could get over that ma'am thing.

Chrissy once again turned the news channel on as she readied herself for her journey. Hearing nothing, she scanned the room, grabbed her backpack, hung the "Do Not Disturb" on the inside door handle, and closed the door behind her.

CHAPTER

14

Chrissy had already filled the fuel tank at Matthew's and discovered there were still no maps. The decision now was to give the southbound route another try or head north. She recalled Kenny mentioning the town she hoped to find when she headed south the last time—a town that did not appear. If it was because of a wrong turn she made, she did not know. So she thought, it may be north.

Chrissy wished she had asked Kenny this morning, but at this point, she did not want to backtrack, even if it was only a few blocks. Distance was her only objective right now. So north it was, although north brought her closer to the core of the original crisis. She knew she also had to fuel the beast, so finding that town was a necessary evil.

This whole area seems to be densely forested with few towns. Having checked the GPS and still gotten no response, along with no local map, heading to known local towns was a necessity.

Her journey through town was the first time she had really seen it in its entirety. She noticed how all seemed so clean and organized. The wonderful collection of unique and quaint little shops. People walking and shopping, greeting and talking.

Next to Hazel and Norm's general store was an antique book store. She noticed a small art gallery, a collection of men's and women's clothing shops, each with creative window displays. There was even a place that sold only fudge, which was a hard one to pass by for Chrissy. It stood next door to a shop named the Nut House.

There was a small teahouse with a few bistro tables and chairs out front. All were taken, with patrons sitting and enjoying the warm sun.

In all, the town looked very prosperous. The whole scene was almost a postcard-perfect image. As her circumstances cleared and maybe after her jail term, she felt she could find her way back for an extended visit, she thought morosely.

Reaching the end of the main—the *only*—street, Chrissy slowed within sight of the church. She recalled how the sanctuary of a church left her with a calm, secure feeling. Although not particularly religious, she felt a sense of a power from it far beyond that of mortal man's. Chrissy recalled Reverend Sounders saying at breakfast that he would be out of the area all day on church business. If the doors were open, this might be the time to do her meditation.

Heading off in a state of confusion was never part of her makeup, but her current predicament had introduced a completely new personality, both of sight and mind.

CHAPTER

15

The town church was a turn-of-the-century-looking clapboard style. It had a small square spire above the two large wooden front doors. Through the louvered openings in the bell tower, Chrissy could see the sun reflecting off a polished bronze bell. Although as with the rest of the town, the church might be old in design, it was as if it had just been newly built with its crisp white finish and detailed fieldstone foundation. The roof was a cedar shake just like there was on the family lake retreat.

Chrissy felt the strong draw to enter the church and spend some time within its walls. Turning into the church parking lot, she drove to the rear to hide her car from view. Entering the unlocked rear church door, she at once felt that blanket of calm cover her. And with the knowledge that this was where she should be right now, she scanned the interior.

Seeing she was alone, Chrissy selected a pew in the center of the small church and sat herself. Locking her fingers together, she leaned forward, placing her forearms on the pew's back in front of her. She then, with closed eyes, rested her head on her hands to search for the meadow she left so abruptly.

Within a few minutes, she was there with the warm sun and the gentle breeze caressing the wildflowers and sweet meadow grasses. Allowing her mind to drain of all her current thoughts and concerns, she concentrated on the formation of the rainbow. As it became brighter and clearer, she was aware of a warmth coming over her, and the thought of Ryan came forward. The thought was of her relationship with him.

She went back to their first meeting that first day. It all seemed so long ago, and at the same time seemed as if it was only a couple of days ago. That first meeting at her house. *The day dad barbequed for us all. The day we welcomed the new neighbors.* That might have been the day that Chrissy's life started the left turn—the turn from the friends at the cottage that had, for the most part, been the base for who she was and what she did. Aside from the wonderful guidance of her family, that is.

The friends at the cottage were open and would be honest and straightforward with her. She felt she could talk with them and realize an answer that she could believe in. Tommy, of course, was the one she trusted the most.

Susie, she was quiet. Her parents of Asian descent led a very calm and gentle life, which Susie was used to and, for the most part, followed. She was slighter in stature, but when she laughed, you could hear her for three cottage roads. It was a high-pitched ratchet laugh with a hiccup at the end of each bout. *Every time she laughed, it got our who group laughing. She is just a treat.* Still of slight build, she had grown into a most beautiful, elegant woman. Her interior fashion business was quickly becoming a household name.

Bobby, he was another story. He was the clown of the group. No matter what silly project or scheme the group was involved in, it was a good chance it was thought up by Bobby.

Like the time he convinced us all to collect cardboard boxes for an entire month. Then we built two boats from them using duct tape to hold them together. The idea was to race them to Snake Island. Chrissy would have no part of going anywhere near anything with the name *snake* in it. Tommy, Sharon, and Bobby crewed one named the *SS Minnow*. Of course Bobby insisted on that name. Allen, Marcus, and Susie crewed the other, which they name *Santa Maria*.

They looked great, and old fence boards made good paddles. Now, in a canoe or kayak, the trip to the island was about a four-minute casual paddle. With all their calculations, they figured that four minutes was plenty of time to get to the island and back. No problem. What they did not consider in those calculations was canoes and kayaks have pointy fronts. The cardboard boats did not. The race began with Chrissy being the starting official. After two minutes, they were about eighteen feet from the shore. Not a good sign.

On top of the blunt-nosed vessels slowing them, the laughter of the crew drew their strength to paddle. At about twenty-five feet from shore, it was evident that the *Santa Maria* was going to be a goner before reaching the new land. But they pushed on. Chrissy had to rush back to her cottage for the washroom from the pressure of laughing too hard. She also thought she should tell her dad to man a lifeboat just in case. It was close, but they all made it to the island.

Dragging what was left of their crafts onto the island, the *SS Minnow* crew was jumping and screaming, "We are the champions of the world!" They were all yelling and waving, except for Susie. She kept lifting her feet, turning, and looking down. She appeared to be high-step marching in one place, twisting and turning.

Chrissy found out later that Snake Island was named that because a Mr. R. B. Snake once owned it. There were no snakes there at all. They did not know that then. When her dad picked them and their boat remains up in his fishing boat, Susie leaped like a frog on a hot plate to get into the boat.

The event drew a lot of neighbors, who were also laughing and cheering.

Then there was Sharon. Sharon may have been the smartest of the group. She was not at the cottage as often as the rest of the group. Her dad was some big shot of a business and traveled a lot. He would like to take his family with him on his trips. Sharon did share some of the more exotic trips, but not too many. She was shy and spent a lot of time just going along with whatever happened. A great sport! Her family moved away just about the time Chrissy met Ryan.

Allen and Marcus were twin brothers. Did they ever look alike! Chrissy thought even their parents, at times, had trouble telling them apart. They used to play tricks to see if the rest of the group would catch on. Marcus once came to our cottage saying he was Allen.

Chrissy's dad had said he needed a hand painting the cottage. Brad was away at Scout camp, and her dad thought he could use another pair of hands. Marcus was out fishing when dad offered Allen twenty dollars for help. It was for the next Saturday morning.

When that day came, Allen had slept in, so then started the war when Allen came and found Marcus with the can of paint. The tug of war ended with her dad's treasured clear-coated natural cedar deck needing a total coat of paint.

The latest news was that the twins had a law practice. If they are still trading places. That will totally confuse their clients.

Then Tommy. Tommy was and is a total treasure. If ever there was the perfect friend, that, for Chrissy, was Tommy. In spite of all the torture Tommy had to endure at her hands, he had remained a tried-and-true friend. It was now almost thirty years they had been that way.

Tommy was the adopted son of Mr. and Mrs. Morton. Their family dynamics was one of complete love and understanding. His birth mother was Mr. Morton's sister, who unfortunately died during childbirth. Her husband, a military man, was away for months at a time. He felt that for Tommy's sake, it would be best if he had a complete family base. This would also allow him to see Tommy at every leave. This had always been an open subject, which has worked out well for everyone.

Chrissy always thought it cool to have two dads. Tommy, though, was really closest with his adoptive dad, whose name was also Tom.

The sister wanted the boy to be named after her loving brother. As it happened, their grandfather's name was Thomas Edward Morton. Taking Tommy in as their own son worked out fine as the Mortons had no other children of their own.

Then there was Ryan. That cute new neighbor. The whole new experience for Chrissy.

Ryan, through his youth, was a young man not afraid of work. He, however, had an overinflated sense of his value. This was not to say he did not do a good job or did not follow through on his commitment. It was just to say that his ego was possibly just a bit too big.

Chrissy's dad had hired him a couple of times to help with projects around the house, times when Brad or Chrissy were busy with other things and unable to help. Small jobs, like when her dad had decided to replace the garden shed with a newer, larger one. Ryan had given her dad the idea that he had almost built a complete house on his own, so a garden shed would be a no-brainer for him. It turned out that he had helped a local contractor. His official position was to hold and carry boards for him.

He, for sure, was a great help to her dad, but his worth and value were more standard than supreme. Chrissy was sure that his accounting of her dad's project to the next employer would be that he designed and built the complete chalet by himself.

You would have to admit that he was—and is—a very fast learner.

All through high school, he took on many different types of jobs. One would assume that was to see which one he thought he would want to pursue on graduation or seek further education for.

The one that seemed to have that greatest draw for him was when he was selling door-to-door items. He found his persuasive powers to be his greatest asset—far greater than his physical ones. He continued along this style of work throughout his senior years. Even on a part-time basis, he made quite a bit of money—enough money to buy himself a new car with cash.

After school, he took a job with an investment firm. As a financial service rep for Fermwell and Powell Investments, Ryan found his ground. He started as a rep in what they call the "boiler room." This was an area where a group of people would do cold calls to advise and convince prospective investors to invest in smaller stocks, referred to as penny stocks. With his natural gift of gab, Ryan did extremely well, and he moved up through the company quickly. Over a three-year period, he worked to attain his CFP (certified financial planner) classification, and after five years, he started his own investment business, Rymore Financial Growth Management.

Chrissy's conscious level became aware of a soft shuffling coming in her direction. She lifted her head from her hands and focused in the direction of the noise. It was Matthew from the garage. His eyes trained on Chrissy, he slowly and quietly headed in her direction.

"I am so sorry to bother you. Are you okay? Well, I mean is your car okay. I saw it out back of the church and just wanted to make sure you were not having any trouble with it."

"No, it is like new again, thanks to you, Matthew."

"Well, I thought you had already left town, and when I saw the car, I was a bit worried there was a problem. So glad to hear all is fine. I was just here putting new flowers on my mom's grave. I replace them every week, but this is the anniversary of her passing, and I wanted to spend a bit more time with her."

"I am so sorry to hear she has gone. She must have been quite young," Chrissy respectfully asked.

"Yes, she was young by today's standards. She was sixty-three. She was busy making plans for all she was going to do when she retired. She worked for a local lawyer as a receptionist. She had been there twenty-two years. She would also help with the paperwork at the garage since Dad died four years ago. Almost four years to the day."

"I am so sorry to hear that, Matthew. Do you have any brothers or sisters?"

"No, Miss Hemmings, I am an only child."

"Oh please, Matthew, call me Chrissy. Are you from here? Your family, I mean. I know you worked with your dad at the garage. Did he start it?"

"Well, my dad had lived his entire life here. He started working for Mr. Ritman at the garage when he was eighteen. Mr. Ritman actually started the garage. That is why the garage is called R Town Service Center. *R* for Ritman. Then my Dad took over the business when Mr. Ritman retired. I worked part-time with Dad all my school life, and when I finished school, I came on full-time. He was a wonderful man and a fantastic mechanic. Now, Mom was something like you, a young lady passing through when she had some car trouble. The rest is history."

"Are you married, Matthew?"

"No, well, not yet. Angela—that's my lady friend—she has been putting some pressure on for the last couple months. She is the perfect girl for me, and I do love her. Just cold feet, I guess." Looking and pointing down, Matthew asked, "May I?"

Chrissy smiled and nodded as Matthew set himself down at the end of the pew in front of her.

"Liz—you know Liz from the diner? Well, she is a very smart lady, and she told me to get off the fence. That true love does not come around every day, so when it shows at your door, invite it in, and lock the door behind it. So I know Angela and I will marry, and I guess, being honest, the cold feet is just an excuse."

"An excuse for what, Matthew? It sounds like Liz's advice is a sound and wise move for you."

"Well, Miss Hemmings—"

"No, Matthew. Chrissy, please."

"Sorry, yes. Well, Chrissy, I think it is to do with my embarrassment for a foolish move I made."

"Oh, sorry, Matthew, if I went too far and spoke out of turn."

"No, Miss Chrissy, it is time that I faced the truth. You see, there was this fellow that came to town. You probably have heard of the type. The real estate and investment get-rich programs. Well, this was a gentleman for the investment side. Low-risk, high-return investments. I was not sure at first, so I only put a small amount in. Things seemed fine for about six months. That was when I made the big mistake.

"Have you ever gone fishing, Miss Chrissy? Well, he was fishing. He gave me checks on my investment for the first while. That was the nibble. So I thought more was better. As a foolish blind man, I went on to invest my savings and the life insurance from my mom's passing. I am too ashamed to admit how much.

"Sadly, it all came crashing down. According to the investment people, the company that the money was sitting in failed, so the loss for me is enough that now I cannot afford a wedding. Angela and I have a lot of friends—friends that we would want to be a part of our momentous day. I can't tell her what a fool I was, so I let her think I just have cold feet.

"I am so sorry, Miss Chrissy. I have never admitted this to anyone before. We do not really know each other, and here I am sharing my problems with you.

"Well, I better get back to it," Matthew explained as he got up to leave. "Mom and Dad's plots are lookin' a little untidy, and I am their gardener. Okay, my—that brings back memories. That investment guy used that in his pitch. 'Let me be your gardener and grow your money tree' or something like that."

Matthew quietly whispered as he headed for the church doors, "Miss Chrissy, you have a safe trip, and please stop in if you are ever back in the area."

Chrissy could only nod with a confused, concerned look as she recognized that quote.

CHAPTER

❧ 16 ❧

C hrissy sat stunned in the church pew. Could it be that all the people she has met in this town are victims to this one investment scam? Victims as she is, but from the totally opposite side.

Her mind ran through what she thought at the time to be an honest, well-put-together program to help the average investor succeed financially.

Chrissy thought back on Ryan's business. His business grew quickly, and he soon had a financial planning assistant. Renting halls in hotels or convention centers, they would hold seminars to inform and recruit new investors. His retention rate would appear to be high.

Chrissy had sat in on a few, and at each, there would be lineups at the sign-up table.

The motto for his company was "Allow me to guide you on the road to financial wealth and well-being."

She can still hear his pitch. He always started with slowly looking around the room and praising them by commenting on what a great-looking group of people they were. Then, "I hope you are all healthy." He would then take a long pause still looking around and seemingly making eye contact with each person. "Well, you know, my friends, with the financial means to do what you want or desire, you are even stronger and healthier.

"How does wealth relate to health? One word—stress. Recent studies show that money, work, and the economy continue to be the most frequently cited causes of stress for Americans. In addition, a growing number of Americans are citing personal health and their family's health as a source of stress. Overwhelming studies prove that the highest cause of stress is money related. Your work, such as job loss and cutbacks. The economy, the shrinking dollar. Your limited dollar buys you less than ever before. Personal and family health costs. Those medical expenses and drugs costs just keep rising.

"Our program is a wealth-to-health program. Who wants to march to someone else's drums? It is time to write your own music—tunes that suit your own wants and desires. A sweet tune that, at the end of each day, puts you to sleep with a smile on your face and self-satisfaction on your mind— self-satisfaction because you allowed me to share with you the secrets behind wealth building and management.

"Of course each and every one of you can do this on your own. But why wait or suffer through the years of trials, losses, and market crashes like the many years that I have spent learning how to avoid those financial pitfalls. The lessons learned and all the time spent—time *well* spent because I discovered the secrets. The secrets to financial freedom. The secrets I now want to share with you, if you will allow me to.

"I want to add you to our growing list of financially independent friends. I want you to sit back and watch that money tree grow. I want you to sit secure under that tree and never again worry of the storm of dollar shortage, market crash, or job loss. Your tree will shelter you from all of that.

"If you allow, I will be your gardener and make sure your tree is strong, healthy, and fruitful.

"Do you want to be financially free? Do you want you and your family to never stress again? Do you want to march to your own music? Do you want you and your family to live a long healthy, wealthy life? Then allow me to be your new gardener, and let's get your tree firmly rooted in the field of wealth and well-being!"

Gardener, Chrissy thought. *Could it be Ryan?* What were the chances for the same type of business and the same phrase? That along with her discovery last month while doing his businesses taxes for the year end.

The year before, while doing the tax returns for Rymore Financial, she found large amounts of money that was accounted as commission on investment deposits. This past year, there was a vast increase in those commissions, but the funds invested did not seem to warrant the figure.

This was what Chrissy wanted to talk to Ryan about when she was going to his home on that last day—that day that she saw the two police cars and two black unmarked SUVs on the road and up onto the lawn of his house.

Chrissy pulled over and stopped half a block away from that event. Unaware of what was happening, she thought it best to sit back and observe from a distance.

What she witnessed was Ryan being escorted out of his house, handcuffed, and four gorilla-sized men in black suits following with file boxes—file boxes that were full of documents with her name on them.

That was the day she thought she had best take a short holiday until she was clear as to what was really happening.

Being amazed with all the people she has met in this one small town that have fallen victim to investment scam, she wondered if it was possible or reasonable to consider that this may be an area that Ryan visited. If he did, could they be referring to that investment person as him?

But now, with that term *gardener*, the evidence was so strong against him. But why do they all seem so familiar to her? She had never been in this town before that she could recall. And if it was with those trips to the cottage, that was so many years ago. Why do they still look so much as she recalls?

Chrissy suddenly had a flashback.

While she was at Ryan's home office one day, he was gloating about his "Wall of Wealth." It was a wall that was full of pictures of Ryan shaking hands with people as they handed over checks. He explained to her how he was going to make everyone in those photos a very rich person. *Those photos!*

Liz, Hazel and Norman, and even Matthew, along with many more she had seen in town. They were all among the large group of photos on that wall. That was why they looked so familiar. She had not met or seen them in person at all.

She was sure of this now. But do they know, or have any idea of her relationship with Ryan? Had he ever mentioned her to them? If so, would they wake up in the middle of the night and recall him mentioning her. Would they then fit the pieces together? Her name was not exactly a common one.

A strange feeling crept over her, as if her whole body was distorted. It was the combination of embarrassment, fear, and an awkwardness. She was embarrassed that her newfound friends were all possible victims to something she unwittingly might have been caught up in. The fear was that this whole situation might now be much more serious and far-reaching than the horror she already thought was looming. And it was awkward to the fact that she had found comfort and solace with people who, only a few days ago, were total strangers—wonderful people whose dreams were crushed by a scam she now found herself to be a part of.

Should she contact Liz and explain her involvement—or actually, her lack of involvement? Or, as with her original thoughts when seeing Ryan escorted from his home, the thought process that followed and her reasoning for her being on the run—that she was guilty through association.

"What to do? Who do I turn to?" she muttered. "How far and how long do I have to run?"

CHAPTER

ᘓ{ 17 }ᘐ

Chrissy sprang to her feet from her nest on the pew. Quietly and with a harried shuffle, she darted toward the door where her car is parked. Throwing open the door, she almost knocked over a gray-haired lady about to enter, a lady she had not seen in town. Without as much as an apology or acknowledgement for her action, she broke into a frenzied run to her car. She recognized calls to her offering assistance, but Chrissy's focus was locking herself in her car and escaping.

Pulling from the church lot to the road, she glanced back at the lady still standing and holding the open door. Her concerned look was typical of everyone Chrissy had met in this town. The kindness and accepting nature was, to her now, something she felt was undeserved.

She had, in her mind, taken advantage of these wonderful people, even if she was unaware at the start. She was still guilty for not seeing the pattern sooner. She had done Ryan's books for three years.

Her mind still whirling, and now out of view from the town, she pulled to the side of the road. Speeding and lacking focus on her driving was the last thing she needed right now.

To be pulled over for any reason, or worse, to lose control and again find herself off the road, maybe this time in worse shape.

Idling at the side of the road, Chrissy flopped her head back on the headrest. Taking long deep breaths, she worked to conjure up all her inner energy. She now needed to focus on her next moves. Struggling with the attempt to remove or at least lessen the thoughts just placed seemed futile. It was best to think everything out and work toward a clear, logical action, even if she had to sit there all morning.

Chrissy's thoughts popped back to when she was fifteen. She recalled how, in a conversation with her mom, she alluded to the fact that she knew everything and had all the answers. Her mother's words again rang out: "Honey, sometimes knowledge is more of a weight than an asset."

Today more than ever before, this has proven to be true. "For what it's worth, maybe ignorance is bliss. Although the newfound information is stressful, I at least now have all the cards dealt, I hope," she mumbled. "Wow, now I'm even talking to myself."

Chrissy's focus was drawn to a distant approaching car heading into town. She recognized it as Reverend Sounder's.

As much as she respected the reverend, this was not the time to see or talk to anyone. Hoping she was undetected, she put her car in drive and pulled back onto the road, allowing him to pass.

As he passed, she caught a glimpse confirming that it was, in fact, the good reverend. His head was tilted back, his glasses were on the end of his nose, and his right hand was waving in the air like he was conducting a symphonic orchestra while he mouthed every word of some operetta.

Oh how she already missed that wonderful little man! With the exception of their very first meeting, he had a way that always made Chrissy smile, even if her current situation only allowed it to be an inner smile. His jolly nature was a treasure.

❧{ 18 }❧

"Truth," Chrissy muttered. "Truth is something we all want, yet sometimes we find hard to accept. I had thought my whole life was built on truth."

Chrissy recalled that time when she was very young and how she was going to make up the story about how someone stole the Valentine chocolates meant for her mother. Even though Granny saved the day once again, she still took her dad aside and explained the truth.

The pressure of knowing she did not come clean on something, for Chrissy, was too uncomfortable, and untruths and deception were never part of her makeup. The consequences for being honest were never as much as what she had to carry had she lied.

Her dad did quietly buy another box for Granny.

What is truth? she thinks, then she recited aloud, "Truth as I know it is the assembly of undisputable facts about any subject that defines that subject. Sometimes the truth can change as new facts come to light. Were the facts all there for me and I missed them? Or were they all there and I suppressed them? Did my relationship with Ryan allow a blindness to come over me as I did his books? He did seem to be very successful very quickly. That does happen, though. What sort of forensic accountant would I be if I allowed my personal feelings to cloud or blind me from the truth? Were the signs all there? Did they seem insignificant till now?

"Now I have met the victims. All the everyday, hard-working people who now have had all their hopes and dreams altered—altered not for just a day, a week, or a year, but altered for the rest of their lives. All that they had worked for, taken forever.

"Has meeting the victims caused a restoration of my vision. An earthquake can cause total destruction and impact lives in an irreversible way. We do feel some pain and sadness for the victims. But only when these victims are close to your heart do you really feel the true consequences of that quake.

"My world has just been shaken up. It is now up to me to repair or make right the damage. I cannot afford to repay. I do not even know how far-reaching this is. But at least I can do what I should have done from the start. Report the issues. That is what a forensic accountant does. So heading home it is. Tell the truth and face the music. This may be music Ryan never thought he would march to."

Chrissy's emotion now has moved from fear and escape to anxiety for disclosure. This was the first time she recalled white lines on the highway on this whole unfortunate trip. They just couldn't pass by fast enough.

Muttering, she started to formulate all the facts and events in her relationship with Ryan. "This will be part of the investigative information. Guilty or not, the whole story must be told."

In the distance, a Rest Area sign came into focus. The sun was starting to set, and Chrissy felt it a good time to stop for the night. Even with a very early start, tomorrow would be a long day's journey home.

CHAPTER

❧ 19 ❧

C hrissy woke to the faint scolding of crows. Raising her head enough to peek out of her sleeping bag over the dash of the car, she saw a fox scurry across the parking area that stopped only for a second to look back at what the crows might be calling about. He then disappeared into the dense bush that surrounded the rest area.

The sun looked warm and inviting as it speared its light through the trees. There was a heavy mist lying just above the ground. Although she was cozy and warm in her cocoon, she could watch each breath drift from her, and there was a chill to the end of her nose.

What a wonderful morning. This was the time of day at the cottage when she would hear Dad rustling around, readying for his so-called fishing thing with Tommy's dad.

Her thoughts turned to her mom, dad, and brother. She thought today might be a good time to call to let them know she was all right and see if there had been anyone there looking for her.

How would she explain herself? What exactly did she know? Ryan's papers that she worked from all seemed in order. He did allow himself a hefty service fee. He did pay out to investors. However, there were some movements of funds to other portfolios that did not do so well, and he did lose money for clients. "I guess the truth is I really do not know all that much. When I saw the removal of him from his house, my assumption was that it was for the investment business. Of course it must be. They had all the client and financial file boxes. Do I really have any evidence to the negative, or are they only suspicions? With his fast talking ways, the large amounts of money he has been flashing, and then the fact that it would appear that it was Ryan who visited this town—from all the information given by Liz and everyone else—it sure seems to point to him."

After a quick freshening up, Chrissy got back on the road. Having her last energy bar with a bottled water while driving, she considered that it was a bit too early to call home. It would be better to call in about an hour. This might be the longest hour of the day.

CHAPTER

❧ **20** ❧

*S*weet, *sweet Tommy. He was someone who had never let
me down, even after the years of torture that I put him
through as a child.*

"Ryan—why did I get involved with Ryan? Right from
the start, I knew he was more into himself than anything
else. Why did I try so hard to be a part of his world when
the world I was living in was working just fine? Does this
go back to the fact of my wanting to win? To take control
of a situation? Or that side of me that needs and looks for a
challenge? Ryan would call and ask me out then later say that
he had forgotten a previous commitment. That scenario has
happened so many times."

Chrissy's head was spinning with thoughts of how
involved she might be in this possible scam being run by
Ryan. Thinking back to companies that Rymore Financial
Growth Management (Ryan) had listed as a debtor, there was
one company that sounded too familiar, Phoenix Financial.

Years ago when Ryan was planning a business venture
during high school, he bounced around a name, Phoenix
Promotions. Was the similarity just a coincidence, or was it a
shell company?

This is only one of what I suspect are false investment maneuvers. Maneuvers that I should have seen. Were those companies that he rolled the clients' funds over to true, legitimate companies or more of his schemes? Why was I so blind? I must be deeper into this than I thought. Still I must move forward and admit that I should have seen the pattern.

I do have to admit that I was proud to be the one he wanted to do his accounting. The thought is now, was I chosen because he felt he could control my actions? It is becoming clearer that the whole relationship was one that was for his betterment. Anything that we did together was something that was his choice. If we went somewhere for a trip, it ended up that there was someone he had to meet or had an opportunity to have them invest.

It was becoming frighteningly clear how he pulled all the strings. He had a wonderful knack of allowing you to feel that it was your idea. He would credit you for coming up with them.

I only now have had my eyes opened, and I have no one to blame but myself. Dad always told me to not find fault with someone else for a decision I made. It is up to me to go into any situation with my eyes open and my mind clear. He also told me to never sign on the dotted line until I had read and completely understood what I was signing.

Well, Dad, my eyes were closed, my mind was unfocused, and I was willing to sign anything he put in front of me.

I now have made the notes, studied the facts, and at last seen the light.

I am so ashamed of my conduct. I am not sure how to tell Mom and Dad. All I can do is tell the truth. No matter what Ryan did, it is me who failed to recognize the signs until I saw the gorillas taking him away. Even then my actions to run must mean that I already was aware—aware of a possible fraudulent act. My subconscious mind told me to escape. This tells me there was suppressed knowledge of what he was doing. Why did I not understand this before now? I guess I was just hoping it would all go away. Well, it hasn't.

That is, I assume it hasn't. There has been no local broadcast of Ryan's arrest.

When I get to the next stop, town, whatever, I must call Mom and Dad to confess what has gone on.

CHAPTER

{ **21** }

For quite a number of the next few miles, Chrissy's head was swimming with events, actions, and dealings of Ryan's business.

Finally she could see in the distance what appeared to be buildings. Her thoughts turned to fueling up and, if there was a restaurant, having a well-needed meal. Then a long conversation with her family.

As she came to the point of confirming what looked like a town, a slight anxiety rushed through her. No matter what her fate, the thought of being home was more of a comfort than what the last weeks have been.

As the buildings became clear, a nervous chill ran through her as she slid her foot off the gas pedal. She allowed the car to coast to the side of the road as she stared, bewildered, at the sight in front of her. There, three buildings ahead on the left, was an all-too-familiar site. Debbie's Diner. Just down on the right was R Town Auto Service, Matthew's garage.

Mouth open, arms straight and her hands strangling the steering wheel, Chrissy stared dumbfounded at the sight. "How? Why? What happened?" were all the words she could muster.

Still in gear, she idled on the side of the road as she stared and stammered. Then, crawling over every driving move she made, she could not recall any area where she would have made a turn. So why was she back on the other end of a town that she left the day before?

Chrissy checked the gas gauge as she puts the car in park. Seeing there was one quarter of the tank remaining, she decided to fuel up at Matthew's and head straight through town to see if there was a turnoff. With the state of mind she was in when leaving the church, she may have missed a turn or cutoff.

She did not want to admit to travelling in a circle to Matthew, but there was no way around the low fuel issue. "Swallow your pride and just do it," she bolstered herself. "Then find that missed turn. This time with full concentration on the road. But before all that, I must call home."

Grabbing her backpack, Chrissy rummaged around for her cell phone. Mumbling "Here it goes, my signal to the world," she switched her phone to On. With the beeping and rattling of tunes as it switched between modes, she could feel her excitement grow. "Finally, a link to the outside world." The past weeks were the first time her phone had been off in the year she has had it.

An excitement built as her eyes followed the lighted face of the main screen and the sequential lines dashing across the top of the screen as it searched for a signal. "Oh no!" she yelped as No Service popped up. "This can't be! Come on, we are not in an uncharted jungle in the middle of Africa. There must be cell service."

Chrissy drove ahead twenty feet, waving the phone in the air, but still got the same results.

The issue with GPS was one thing, but now the phone? She recalled the time that she and her mother were at a fall fair. This was before her brother Brad was born, so she reasoned she must have been around two. The sights and sounds were so exciting that she did not pay attention to her mother. When she came back to the point of wanting to take Mom's hand, there was no Mom in sight. That same terror was relived. She felt totally lost and abandoned. All she had to do then was to turn around and find her Mom four feet behind, smiling. No chance of that today. "I am all alone here, and it's up to me to find my way home again, alone."

Chrissy headed for the gas station while deciding to do a bit of touring of the roads on the north end of town again. She must have missed that turn. So once she found it, she would grab something to eat and get some rest before heading out again—this time with full knowledge of the proper route.

CHAPTER

22

Fortunately for Chrissy, Matthew was not at his station when she stopped. She was attended to by a man she did not recall seeing before. This was a good thing. Another embarrassing moment avoided for now.

Filled with fuel and still with no maps or GPS, she headed out of town in search of that elusive road home.

Passing the church, she saw Reverend Sounders in the front garden area talking to the woman she almost knocked over with the church door. Chrissy could only assume that it was Mrs. Sounders. When she came back from finding the correct road, she felt she should apologize for her actions.

Thinking that she would have to go back to town for the night, she wondered what she could say and how she would be able to face anyone. "I guess while I am coming clean, if I see Liz, I should also confess where I fit into her financial woes."

Chrissy has always felt confession was the better of any situation, but this is the biggest hole she had ever fallen into. This was also the most relief she had ever felt for an admission of guilt. She had resolved to face whatever may befall her.

Now, with all her concentration on the road, she left town. Her center of attention was for any signs or indications of a cutoff or a side road.

It was only a short drive out of town when she noticed that just ahead on the left was a sign. Looking at the size and location, it would most likely be the town sign. She often wondered what the name stood for. Possibly an Indian name or a native word for the area.

As she passed, she checked the rearview mirror to confirm. What she saw caused her to slam on the brakes in the middle of the road. "This can't be!" she blurted. "This must be a dream . . . a nightmare." She then turned to look at the town sign, then looked again in the rearview mirror.

No cell service. No GPS service. No maps. Is this a coincidence? Each time I leave, it is only a trip back to where I started.

Everyone in this town would appear to be a victim of Ryan's scams—scams she had to atone for. Was this all part of a trap she had to live in?

Turning again to look in the mirror, she felt the terror of never going home again.

Coming soon, Part 2

Chrissy's confusion and fear mount with new terror as she desperately searches for an escape from what seems to be a never ending nightmare.

Soon to be released

Escape from TUOYAWON

ABOUT THE AUTHOR

The creativity of R. Murrey Haist (www.haist.artist-websites.com) encompasses a broad range. He is internationally recognized for his award-winning paintings, airbrushing, photography, and pyrography. His poetry has been published in books and magazines.

His creative artistic work has been featured on television, on permanent display in archival-museum-galleries, and is recognized throughout North America and Europe. That same creative mind has now produced this cliff hanger mystery series also destined for international acclaim.

Lightning Source UK Ltd.
Milton Keynes UK
UKHW01f1935150618
324325UK00001B/90/P